WHO I WAS WITH HER

WHO I WAS WITH HER

NITA TYNDALL

HARPER TEEN
An Imprint of HarperCollinsPublishers

HarperTeen is an imprint of HarperCollins Publishers.

www.epicreads.com
ISBN 978-0-06-297838-7
Typography by Jessie Gang
20 21 22 23 24   PC/LSCH   10 9 8 7 6 5 4 3 2 1

❖

First Edition

For the girls who hide their hearts.

THE DAY OF.

When I hear that she's dead, I run.

I hear it from the girls in the locker room. It threads through their conversation so carelessly, *did you hear a girl from Leesboro died* weaving through talk of which girl gave a blow job to Jack Morris behind the bleachers and who's going to Matt's party this weekend.

The thread of it snags in my gut, because Leesboro was Maggie's school.

It's not her, I tell myself. *It can't be her or someone would have told me; her brother would have called me; someone—*

But she didn't answer her phone this morning.

And last night she didn't text me good night, and I brushed it off because she's tired from training, we're seniors and we're all so goddamn tired—

But I have to know.

"Which girl?"

I hear myself asking it and I hear how hoarse my voice is and

I know I'm giving myself away but I have to know—

"Which girl?"

I push my way through everyone until I find Haley Russell, because she's always the first to know any gossip.

"Jesus, Corinne, calm down," she says, staring at me. "I mean yeah, it's sad, but—"

Julia Recinos, our captain, steps between Haley and me because she knows how we are. "It was their captain," she says.

Maggie.

Oh, God, it was Maggie. The girl I—

But Julia doesn't know that. None of them can know that; none of them can know we were dating.

"Corinne, are you okay?" Julia asks, but I can barely hear her because all I can think is Maggie, my Maggie, is dead, and none of these girls will ever know what she meant to me.

I should be hiding how I'm feeling but I can't, so I push through Julia and Haley and I fight my way out of the locker room and I do what I always do—

I run.

ONE YEAR BEFORE.

I am going to lose this race.

I know I'm not the best runner. I'm not Julia or Haley or Valerie the freshman, faster than all of us. I am a middle-of-the-pack outsider who doesn't know what she's doing, only running because Julia convinced me to try out when I moved here almost a year and a half ago.

But this girl from Leesboro. She's not a middle-of-the-pack outsider, you can tell by the way she runs. Her curly ponytail, secured by a lime-green scrunchie, has swung ahead of me for three meets, signaling how much faster she is than me.

I don't know why, but it's starting to be annoying.

I push myself. Just a little, just enough to catch up to her, still far behind JuliaHaleyValerie and the other girls who deserve to be here. She glances at me, sharing a conspiratorial smile before speeding up again, passing me, moving toward the front like she has the past few races.

She's going to win. Again.

There are cheers as she crosses the finish line, cheers again as I know either Julia or Haley has crossed it.

And I'm in the middle, like always.

I'm breathing hard, so I turn away from my coach and the other girls running in and find a quiet place to stretch. Somewhere in the crowd is my dad, cheering me on loudly like it'll make up for the fact Mom didn't come.

I don't know why I look for her anymore.

I bend down and grab the toes of my shoes, stretch, lean forward through the pain because it'll be worse later if I don't. Breathe in. Out.

And then there's a shoe next to mine. Bright pink, muddy cross-country spikes. My eyes roam up a pair of pale, freckled legs, and then look up to see the girl from Leesboro, her face flushed.

"Hi," she says, and her voice is a soft Southern lilt I'm still not used to. "Mind if I stretch here?"

I switch legs. "Sure."

"Sure you mind?" she asks, and laughs. My face grows hot, and it isn't because I just got done running.

"Sure you can stay. I don't mind," I say, and she smiles before leaning down to stretch.

"You ran good," she says after a minute. "Almost caught me at one point. That's what, two times now?"

"Three," I say, and she laughs again.

"Three. Maybe next time it'll be four." She grins at me,

and when she does, her whole face scrunches up. "Guess you should know my name, then, if you keep catching up to me. I'm Maggie."

"Corinne," I say, taking her hand as she pulls me up to stand. We're left staring at each other.

Does she hold on for just a second too long? Or am I imagining that?

"I guess I'll see you at the next meet, then?" she says.

Is there something hopeful in her voice?

"Guess you will," I say.

There's the same note of hope in mine.

THE DAY OF.

She's gone.

Those are the words going through my head as I run the trail behind our high school, branches and leaves whipping my arms and my hair, and I don't even care if I'm getting scratched because I need to feel something because Maggie is *gone*—

A sob escapes my throat before I can stop it, and I hope I'm deep enough in the woods that no one can hear me.

She's gone. It doesn't feel real, and maybe it isn't; maybe they meant another girl, a captain of another cross-country team named Maggie, because my Maggie can't be dead.

But I know. Deep in the pit of my stomach, I know. She didn't call me last night and she didn't text me this morning and it is because she is dead. She's dead and no one knows about us—God, no one knew we were dating or that we were even friends, and now, now they won't know, now they can't, because I can't tell anyone without her here with me.

I stop running, panting, and I don't know if it's from grief or what and I bend over with my hands on my knees and that awful aching in my chest, waiting for something, some kind of release, but it's not coming—

Maggie's gone.

I just saw her. I *just* saw her and how can this girl I loved be—

I bite my lip so hard I taste blood.

This isn't fair. This isn't fucking fair it isn't Maggie's *gone* Maggie's dead—

I press my hand to my mouth.

"Corinne?"

Leaves crunching, and I look up and it's Julia, concern on her face, and then guilt stabs at me even more because Julia was my first friend here, my *best* friend, and she doesn't know about me and Maggie and I want so desperately for her to comfort me but how can she? When she doesn't know?

"Are you okay?" she asks.

What a ridiculous question. My girlfriend is dead. I don't know if I'll ever be okay again.

But Julia doesn't know because I didn't tell her, I didn't want to tell anyone, and so I nod.

"I'm fine."

"Did you know her?"

Did I know her?

What do I say?

Of course I know her, I know everything about her. I know

that her curly hair turned frizzy in the summer from North Carolina humidity, know that ever since she was six she wanted to be Christine in *Phantom of the Opera* even though she couldn't sing, know that she liked sprinkles in her hot chocolate but hated marshmallows. Know that she went to church every Sunday without fail.

I know she wanted to tell her parents, I know how her lips felt against mine and how easy it was to get my fingers tangled in her hair when we kissed and how she looked when she told me she loved me, I know I knew—

But I can't tell Julia that. Any of it.

"I mean," I say, because I have to say something, "I knew her from running, and I'd seen her around, but—"

She's looking at me, staring at me hard, because Julia would have known Maggie from running, too, and it doesn't mean anything to her because she clearly isn't upset—

"I didn't know her," I say, and pick myself up and walk away before she can stop me.

My phone doesn't buzz as I get in my car. There's no text from Maggie asking if we can meet after practice, nothing asking if I have work this weekend because she wants to hang out. Nothing but a silence that stretches as empty as I feel on the inside.

I turn my phone off. Julia won't text me, and if my phone is off I won't be tempted to scroll through all of my conversations with Maggie, the photos of us I have saved in a secret app; I can ignore the fact that it won't chime with a new text from her. If I turn it off I won't spend all night replaying her voice mails over and over, looking up the gruesome facts of her death that I know must be out there. If my phone is off I won't have to think about how no one is going to call and console me, because no one knew we were dating.

Fuck.

Blue light from the TV flickers behind the curtains as I pull up, our cat Bysshe's fat frame silhouetted in the window, jumping down when my headlights catch him. I know the second I open the front door he'll try to make a break for the crawl space even though now he's too fat to fit under there.

I hoist my backpack over one shoulder and my gym bag over the other, open the door, and immediately bend down to scoop Bysshe up and kiss the top of his head.

I can't believe Dad named the cat after Percy Shelley. But that's my dad. IT guy by day, reading Lord Byron by night. I grew up listening to Shelley's poetry and Mary Shelley's *Frankenstein* instead of bedtime stories, the desire to take things apart to see how they worked already sprouting.

"I'm home," I say, stepping into the living room where my dad is sitting with a TV tray and a plate full of pasta. Like nothing's changed, like this is a normal weekday night. Like my world hasn't shifted off its axis.

I clutch Bysshe tighter to me and he squirms in protest before I set him down along with my bags, heading to the kitchen.

"How was practice?" Dad asks.

"Fine," I say. "What's for dinner?"

"Chicken alfredo," he says. "So practice was fine? Think it'll be a good season? How're you feeling about it? It's a big year, Corey."

I wince at the barrage of questions, grateful he can't see. "I know," I say. "But it's too early to tell right now anyway."

My runner's nutrition sheet is taped to the fridge, where it's been since I started running. Dad takes it more seriously than I thought he would—the running. When I told him Julia had asked me to join the team, he immediately drove both of us to the local sporting goods store to buy spikes and gear and even sports bras, because Julia knew what we needed and neither my dad nor I did. He printed out my nutrition sheet and made me all the meals and timed me running around the neighborhood and watched me train, and I want to think it's because he's proud of me, but part of me knows it's because he's dreaming of athletic scholarships, dreaming of the day I'll get out of here.

It's not like we wanted to come to North Carolina. Dad's parents are from here and he always talked about hating it, hating how everyone knew everyone's business, so when he met Mom, all the way from the Colorado mountains, he jumped at the chance to leave.

But we moved back here two years ago because Nana got

sick, and then Mom's drinking got worse and the divorce happened and Nana died and now we're all stuck here, ten miles
and a tense phone call away from Mom.

I know why he wants me to leave. I get it. It's the same feeling I always get, that *I do not belong* no matter how much I
pretend to. Dad may be able to slip into his accent when he
needs to charm someone, but more often than not he doesn't.
We don't go to church. We don't like NASCAR, or football, or
have a pig pickin' for our Christmas party like Maggie's family
does. Dad left our small town behind when he finished college
and he fully expects me to do the same. To my dad, running is
my ticket out of here.

Running was *our* ticket out, mine and Maggie's, but I can't
think about that right now.

I scoop some chicken and pasta out of the pot on the stove,
don't even bother to heat it, and drift back into the living room
just as Dad switches to the news.

And there she is.

I almost drop my bowl because I can't believe it but there is
Maggie's senior portrait and there is her car wrapped around
a tree and there is her name on the screen and on this news
anchor's lips, another pretty high school girl gone too soon.

Dad turns up the volume and with it the knife of grief twists
a little further in my gut.

"They're saying she was a runner. Did you know her?" he

asks, not knowing what this question is doing to me.

I swallow, turn and walk into the kitchen, pretend I didn't hear him as I open the fridge and stick my head in.

Maybe if I stay here, I'll freeze so much my heart will stop and I'll be able to pretend Maggie isn't dead.

"Corinne?"

"No," I say, for the second time that day. "No, I didn't."

Bysshe follows me up the stairs, purring loudly as he jumps onto my bed and curls up at the foot. I give him a treat from the bag I keep under the bed and flop down next to him.

I should have told. I should have come out, I should have—

I pick up my phone and turn it on, contemplate calling Dylan, because he's the only person I have left now, the only one who knew about me and his sister.

I should call him. I should tell him I'm sorry for his loss, I should talk to someone who loves (loved) her, who knows I love her, too, but I can't bring myself to pick up the phone.

I did this to myself.

ONE DAY G O N E.

For a second when I wake up, I forget.

And I roll over and I reach for my phone because there'll be a text from her saying she wants to hang out after the meet this weekend and—

But there's nothing.

My chest feels hollow. Is hollow.

Maggie's gone, Maggie's dead, Maggie died—

And I have nothing physical to remind me of her, nothing tangible, and suddenly I desperately want a piece of her to hold on to. What will her family do with her running stuff? Her spikes, her shorts, her medals? Where do they go, the belongings of a dead girl? Will her parents keep her room the way it was so she'll be seventeen forever, a girl trapped in the glass box of other people's memories?

I need her running stuff. I need to see it, need to have it because it's a reminder of who we were, what we were to each other, how we met, and I need to have it, not sealed up in her closet forever.

Without thinking, I pull out my phone to text Dylan.

Where's Maggie's running stuff? I type, then stop myself. Because why should I get her stuff? Why do I deserve it, over Dylan? Over her family? Who the fuck am I to demand Maggie's stuff the day after she died, from her brother who's grieving, her brother I don't even know that well—

I erase the message with shaking hands and just type **I'm sorry** to him, send it, though I know those two words can't even begin to encompass who Dylan has lost.

Who I've lost.

Fuck.

I don't know how I make it through school.

I keep expecting everyone to talk about it, talk about her, but she didn't go to our high school, so why would it matter that she's dead? Why would anyone care about the girl from our rival school who died?

I want them to care. I want them to care because I do, because this is shattering me slowly from the inside and if they cared maybe it wouldn't be so goddamn lonely.

There are a few hushed whispers in the hallway, more in awe over the fact someone close to our age died than anything. We think we're invincible until we're not, and at the same time, there's relief in the air, an awful kind of relief.

At least it wasn't one of us.

I make it through Art and I make it through chemistry but by the time we get to English, reading passages from *Jane Eyre* out loud, I can barely hold it together. I sit next to Julia and mindlessly doodle in my notebook, anything to get my mind off Maggie. When class ends, I'm the first to bolt out of my seat, relieved that the day is over.

"Corinne, wait!" Julia says as I head into the hallway. I stop by my locker and turn to her.

"What?"

She stops. "I just . . . are you *sure* you're okay?"

Her question almost makes me start crying.

Almost.

But I can't lose it now, not in front of her, not after yesterday.

"I'm fine," I say, and she narrows her eyes at me.

"Corinne."

I swallow past the lump in my throat. "It—I don't know, hearing about Ma . . . that girl, I just thought about Nana, and . . ."

Julia's face instantly softens. "Oh, Corey," she says, and pulls me into a hug.

Guilt gnaws at my insides because what the *fuck*, Corinne, using your dead grandmother to not tell Julia about Maggie? Who does that?

God, I don't deserve to be grieving her. Not at all.

"I'm fine, I just . . . need some time," I say. "And I might—I might miss practice for a day or two."

Julia nods. "I'll tell Coach. Call me if you need me, okay?" she says, and she hugs me again.

She is so genuine, so *nice*, and if I don't deserve my grief, then I definitely don't deserve Julia's kindness. Or her friendship.

"I will," I say, and she pulls back, my sadness mirrored in her own face, because we both know I probably won't.

FIVE MONTHS BEFORE.

We're in her basement. We were playing pool, but we aren't anymore. Instead, we're on her couch, kissing.

Kissing her is different from kissing any boy. Kissing her is soft hands and soft lips and curves that mirror my own, and hands sliding up shirts and—

"Maggie?"

We break apart, and at the top of the stairs is her brother. Dylan. I've only met him a few times, and he's been nice enough, if a bit wary of me.

His face is as red as his hair.

"You didn't answer when I came in, so I thought you might be down here . . ."

"Dylan," Maggie says, and she's blushing as much as he is. "This is Corinne. My . . . girlfriend, I guess," she says, and it's the *girlfriend* part that fills the room but the *I guess* part that fills me.

Dylan nods, then, turns and heads up the stairs. I tug the

edge of my shirt down and don't look at Maggie, because we've been so careful, we were always so careful—

"He's going to tell."

"He's not."

"He will—"

"No, he won't."

Her hand over mine, my head on her shoulder. I should get up and leave before her brother comes back, but I can't make myself.

But she holds my hand, she keeps me tethered so I can't run away.

ONE DAY G O N E.

I text Julia when I get home, just to say something, to thank her for today. Dad's already in the kitchen when I walk in, cooking. Ground beef is sizzling in a pan on the stove, and I smell the spice blend he uses for tacos. Bowls of toppings are set out on the counter.

Taco night. Like we used to do back when my parents were still together, Dad making tacos and drinks for him and Mom, some sort of fancy mocktail for me.

I pull my hair back from my face, secure it with a hairband around my wrist. Blond strands get caught in my fingers as I pull my hair through the elastic, lean in to sneak a taste of the salsa in the food processor on the counter. I am not much taller than my Dad. We even look alike—same blond hair, same straight noses, though my eyes are brown like Mom's.

I wonder if he hates that—that I got her eyes.

I guess I'd hate it if I were him.

"I'll make you a mocktail if you want," Dad says as he turns off the burner. "Blender's clean. Want a piña colada?"

I swallow.

The last Taco Tuesday night we ever did ended in Mom drinking three piña coladas by herself before we'd even eaten, Dad tight-lipped going to his office to ignore the problem after she passed out on the couch.

I'd brought the leftovers to school the next day and shared them with Chris and Trent and Julia, and when I got home and tried to talk to Dad about what had happened the night before, he just shook his head.

"Sure," I say. "That sounds great."

I shower before dinner, trying to scrub not telling Julia and Maggie's death and my text to Dylan from my mind, as if a shower is going to make any of this go away.

Bysshe is desperately meowing at my bathroom door when I get out, so I give him a treat. When I head downstairs, Dad's already eaten, so I make a taco and sit down at the kitchen table.

Dad's left the newspaper carelessly flipped to the obituary section, and Maggie's senior portrait looks up at me.

I flip it shut so fast I rip the paper and spill half my taco on the ground, plastic plate clattering on our tile floor.

"Everything okay, Corey?" Dad asks.

"Everything's fine," I call back, scooping up filling from the floor and dumping it in the trash.

My hands grab the newspaper before I can stop them,

shoving the pieces in the pocket of my sweatpants. I wet a few paper towels and wipe the floor, throw my plate in the sink, and run upstairs.

On my bed I piece together the newspaper. I don't know why I'm doing this to myself, don't know why I'm going to torture myself reading Maggie's obituary because it'll just be dry facts about how great she was, all the people who have survived her when she should have lived a much longer life than she did—

And yet.

I flatten the scraps, wince when I see I'm getting sauce on top of my purple comforter. I scrape at it with a fingernail, steel myself to read the obituary.

Margaret Jean "Maggie" Bailey.

Maggie Bailey was a senior at Leesboro High School—

Oh god, I can't do this. I can't even look at the dates.

I close my eyes for a moment, try to steel myself, and then open them again. Run my finger down the column until I find the information about the wake.

I have to go. Don't I? I owe it to her to go.

How can I, though? How can I go to her wake knowing that no one there knows who I am? That they get to openly grieve and mourn, and I—

Fuck. It's not like they'll be paying attention to me, anyway, not like everyone will immediately sense that I don't belong. Even in a town as small as ours, that's not going to happen.

I crumple the newspaper and throw it in the trash. Bysshe

jumps up and nudges my hand, and I want to scream at him to get out but instead I bury my face into his fur. He tolerates it for about two seconds, then leaves.

"Corinne?" My dad calls up the stairs. "Where did the paper go?"

"Bysshe tore it. I threw it away," I say, and the cat looks at me, almost affronted. "Sorry."

I hear my dad mutter something about *that damn cat* and my heart races like I've just stopped running.

What if he pieces it together?

But he won't. He has no reason to, he won't.

I press the heels of my palms into my eyes, the pressure stopping me from crying. I think again about texting Julia, Dylan, someone to go to the wake with me tomorrow, but Julia doesn't know and Dylan has to be with his family and I'm going to have to get through this alone.

TWO DAYS G O N E.

My car rumbles as I pull into the parking lot of Whitewood United Methodist. I am the first one here. I turn my car off; shaking hands take keys out of the ignition. I pull my cross-country jacket on over my navy dress, because Maggie hated black and loved to run and I need something that reminds me of her to get through this fucking wake.

I hope it's not open casket.

My phone beeps.

Hope you're doing okay.

Julia.

I almost asked her to come with me, almost thought about explaining to her in the car, but I couldn't bring myself to do it. Couldn't bring myself to tell her that the reason we didn't hang out over the summer is that oh, by the way, I had a secret girlfriend that I was with for almost a year and never told you about, and now she's dead and do you want to come to the wake with me?

I turn my phone off, sit in silence until the Baileys pull up. I want to turn my head away from them, don't want to watch as Mr. Bailey guides Mrs. Bailey out of the car, both of them crumpled, both of them aged fifty years. But Dylan catches my eye and he holds it until they turn to enter the church and oh God, I cannot do this.

If I go in, it'll be final. Maggie will be dead and Dylan will look at me like he hates me and the Baileys won't know how much I loved their daughter. If I go in, all anyone will see is some girl who probably knew Maggie from school, and I will be surrounded by everyone else's grief and not allow any of it for myself, and I just—I can't.

I don't go in.

I sit in my car the entire time, let the car run until the heat fogs up the windows and no one can see that I'm not crying.

There's a rap on my window after the wake is over, a shock of red hair through blurred glass—Dylan.

I can't look at him. I can't look at him because when I do I will see her face.

This was a mistake. Coming here was a mistake.

Dylan raps on the window again and I roll it down just a little, still not looking at him.

"Corinne," he says. "I, um . . . I looked for you."

"I didn't go in," I say.

"I know. I can see that," he says, and absurdly, I want to laugh.

I finally turn my head, just enough to see him. His face is pale, even paler than his normal fair skin, blanched under his freckles.

He looks like her. That's my first thought, that he looks like her except his hair is bright red instead of her brown, his face sharper and more defined. She called him Ron if she was being affectionate—because of the hair. I thought it was his middle name until she told me it was a Harry Potter reference.

I'd been planning to read those books, eventually, but now it just seems pointless. I don't want to read about magic if it can't bring her back.

"Did you—do you want something from me?" I ask, because I can't think of anything else, because here is the only other person who knows about me and Maggie and the only reason he and I are even talking to each other right now is—

Is because she's gone.

He doesn't answer my question, instead responding with one of his own. "Why didn't you go in?"

Because she's gone and it's final and you're the only one who knows and I can't deal with that, I can't deal with her being gone—

Because everyone else is grieving her and I can't because—

Too many ways to tell him that he won't understand, that he *can't* understand. She was his sister and she was my girlfriend but only one of us gets to claim her now that she's gone.

My mouth is dry when I finally answer him. "Do you think I want to see her in there when—"

When she's gone and it's final—

"When no one knows who I am?"

Dylan swears and steps back for a minute, then comes back to my car, placing his hand on the window as if he can push it down farther. "I can't believe you're making this about you. What, you think anyone is going to recognize you? You made sure that didn't happen."

I flinch. "You asked," I say dully.

But he's right and I hate that he is.

If no one recognizes you at your girlfriend's funeral, were you ever really her girlfriend?

"Anyway," Dylan continues, now staring straight at me. "I actually—I need you to come with me. There's someone I want you to meet."

I shake my head. "No."

"Corinne," he says. "You—you owe this to me, okay? To her. Please." His voice is raw when he says the last words. "Trust me."

I get out of the car. Dylan steps back and the two of us start off across the parking lot toward a blue pickup truck, now one of the only cars left.

"How . . . how are your parents doing?" I ask him, and he sighs.

"Not good. I—I'm probably going to take a week off from school to stay here and help them."

"Oh."

A nicer girl, a girl who is not me, would offer to help. That girl would be friends with her girlfriend's brother, her girlfriend's parents; that girl would have people to share her grief with.

But I'm not, and I don't.

We stop in front of the blue pickup. Dylan shoves his hands into his pockets. A girl comes around from the back of the truck, stubbing out a cigarette under her boot. Her skin is a warm brown, her face sharp and angular. Her short hair is shaved on the sides, close dark curls at the top. She's in dark jeans and a button-down top, and she's taller than me even though I'm in heels.

"Who's she?" I ask, my voice as cold as I can make it because if I have to do this, I will be as fucking difficult as he thinks I am.

"This is Elissa. We're friends," Dylan says, gesturing awkwardly to her.

Elissa sticks out her hand. "Hey. Didn't see you inside."

"I didn't go in."

She raises an eyebrow, and I'm about to turn and ask Dylan how he knows her and what he thinks he's doing, when she interrupts me and asks him first.

"Why are you doing this, Dylan?"

He shrugs, then. "You two have something in common.

Thought you could talk about it."

I frown. Elissa doesn't, though. Elissa throws back her head and laughs and says "*That's* her? You're kidding," and my face goes red and Dylan blushes, too.

"What the fuck is happening?" I ask, turning between them. "Dylan?"

He holds up his hands, backs away. "I have to go," he says hastily, and before I can say anything else, he's off, sprinting away from us and into his car at the end of the parking lot.

Elissa turns to me. "So. You too, huh?"

"Me too, what?" I say, though my stomach flips when she asks because I already know the answer.

"You dated Maggie, too."

That answer.

I can't open my mouth to say yes, I did, so I just nod.

She doesn't ask my name, or how long Maggie and I dated, or what high school I go to like anyone else would have. She pulls a pack of cigarettes out of her pocket and offers one to me.

"Nervous habit," she says apologetically. "Want one?"

"No thank you," I say.

"Mind if I . . . ?"

"Actually yeah," I say, even though I don't, because I'm feeling spiteful that Dylan's making us talk and that this girl clearly knows so much about me that she doesn't even need to ask my name.

I say as much. "I got your name, but . . ."

"You're Corinne. I know who you are," she says. And before I can protest, she goes ahead and lights the cigarette anyway. "Maggie told me."

Hearing Maggie's name out of this girl's mouth when I didn't even know Maggie'd dated another girl is enough to steal the breath from my lungs.

"Well, she didn't tell me about you, so . . ."

I should regret what I just said but I can't. Suddenly I'm angry, furious with this girl and with Maggie because why didn't she tell me about Elissa? It's not like she didn't know I'd dated boys before dating her, not like I hadn't spent the better part of sophomore year hanging off Jeremy Hayes's arm and three months off Trent Moore's before her, so why wouldn't she tell me about Elissa?

"You don't go to Leesboro, do you?" I say, just to find out more about her, just to have something to say.

"I did. That's how we met—me and Maggie," she says, like she needs to clarify. "I graduated two years ago."

"What . . ."

"I go to Wake Tech, if that's what you're asking," she says, and there's a note of bitterness in her voice. "Not all of us were planning on Villanova."

"She told you?"

Elissa raises her eyebrows. Of course she'd told her.

"Look," she says, stomping out her cigarette, "I know how hard this must be for you—"

"You don't know shit. I just met you. How are you supposed to know how I feel?" Some part of my brain tells me that of course she knows, she dated Maggie, but I'm too angry to care, because she knew about me when I didn't know about her.

"Corinne—"

"Elissa. I appreciate the concern, but my girlfriend is dead, okay?" My voice cracks. "She's dead and she's not coming back, and nothing some ex of hers says to me is going to make me feel better. So I appreciate Dylan throwing us together, but I don't need you right now."

Elissa's face falls, but she shrugs. "Okay. Fine. I'll see you at the funeral, then? If you've changed your mind by then we can talk."

"Fine," I say, and stalk off toward my car.

I don't look back at her.

ONE YEAR BEFORE.

I look for her the next time we race against Leesboro. My palms are itching; I'm bouncing back and forth from foot to foot. I'm never this nervous before a race, and it shows.

"You're going to burn all your energy before we even start," Julia says, but she's amused.

"I know." I shoot her a grin. "Not like it matters. We both know you're going to pull us to victory."

"Oh, hush," Julia says, but she nudges me with her shoulder before leaning down to stretch. "You're coming over tonight after pasta, right?"

"Obviously," I say, and I bend down beside her. "You've already picked out a movie, right?"

"You know it. *And* there's a giant box of chocolate with your name on it."

"You're the best," I say as I finish my last stretch. When I stand up, Maggie catches my eye from across the line, determination on her face.

I haven't been able to stop thinking about her since our last race. About seeing her again, running next to her, stride in stride.

Why have I been thinking about that?

The bell goes off. This is a mid-season race, nothing too strenuous, yet we're starting to get serious now because of Regionals. This is where it starts to matter.

I'm already ahead, shooting out of the starting line like I haven't since tryouts, because I need to catch up to her. I need to beat her. I need to win.

I pass Haley, pass Julia, hear the breaths of other runners behind me, the crunch of new autumn leaves under our sneakers, the rhythm of my own steps. None of it matters, because I haven't caught up to her yet.

I finally see her ahead of me, lime-green scrunchie signaling me.

She is not going to beat me this time.

I push myself, *run faster run harder be better* because I need to win. I need to see the look on her face when I win.

But I'm not used to this, my body isn't used to running this hard, and I quickly fall back to the middle, because she is so much faster. I almost got close to her, but she is still so, *so* much faster than me, and I can't catch up.

"Corinne!"

I'm stretching by a tree when she calls my name, and when I

lift my head she's already settling herself in the dirt beside me.

"Good race," I say, and she nods.

We're silent for a moment as we lean down and stretch, comfortable companionship.

"Hey," she says after a minute. "Would you wanna . . . I mean, would you wanna get coffee in Raleigh sometime? Like. Hang out outside of races?"

I blink. Surely I haven't heard her right. She's from a rival school, and by all counts we're supposed to be enemies.

But there's something about her. Even though we've barely spoken, there's something about her that makes me think she might be one of the few people in this entire state who would actually understand me.

"Yeah, sure," I say. She beams.

"Great! I'll put my number in your phone, okay?"

I hand her my phone without thinking, stop stretching, watch as she keys her number in.

"Text me," she says, handing my phone back to me and standing. I look down. She's put in her name, Maggie Bailey, and a little smiley face next to it.

"I will," I say, and I watch as she leaves.

TWO DAYS G O N E.

"I was out with Julia," I call to Dad as I come in the door, hurrying up the stairs before he can even ask me how Julia's doing.

I toss my dress off and it lands on Bysshe, who meows in protest before hurrying under my bed. I lie down and pull out my phone, open it to Instagram, to Maggie's page. She kept it locked, but she let me follow her, even put a photo of us up once.

I click on her most recent photo, a shot of her with her hand on her chin, her face like she's clearly trying not to laugh, captioned *wondering if I can convince my team to run to Coney Island Ice Cream for free ice cream?*

View all 458 comments

I start scrolling.

i can't believe i'm never going to see your smile again.

rest in peace girl.

i know God needed you but i wish it wasn't so soon.

i miss you and love you maggie seems like yesterday
you were letting me borrow your romeo and juliet notes.
rip xoxo

theyre dedicating the rest of the season to you,
beautiful.

Anger suddenly flares in my chest. These people, they don't know Maggie, don't know her like I do—did. But here they are commenting on her posts and talking like they were all best friends; they're dedicating everything to her, their grief gets to be public, and they get sympathy and free passes to the counselor's office, and I'm sitting here falling apart and it won't change shit.

I close the app. Before I can stop myself, I open Facebook, even though I rarely use it. Maggie and I were friends, but she only had a profile for her grandparents to see it, and I only had one for updates from a few people in Colorado.

I go to her wall.

It's almost worse, here, the comments, because here are her parents and here are older people from her church, calling her an angel and talking about how she's up in Heaven with her pretty white angel wings. Half the people posting have changed their profile pictures to themselves and Maggie, her face staring out at me from so many tiny circles.

I can't look away.

I switch back to her Instagram, scroll back to the photo of

us, taken together after her school's talent show that she helped manage. My arm around her waist, both of us grinning. I'd been so nervous about her posting it, but girls do that all the time, that casual touching, arms linked or around waists or shoulders. And she wanted to post it, so.

There are no comments on this photo, and I tap to leave one.

What do I say?

What can I say? I can't talk about how much she meant to me or how much I love her or how sometimes we would do homework together and I'd get so absorbed in my work she'd tease me about it, call me a nerd. How she hated her legs because they were too thick and muscular but how I'd spend hours trailing my lips over them, how the knowledge she'd wait for me after a meet so we could go out for a private date was sometimes the only thing that kept me happy. How the first time we had sex she was all I thought about the entire day, how we were both shy because it was the first time we'd really seen each other naked but how even though we fumbled through it, I thought it was perfect. How even though she swore she couldn't sing, my favorite thing was to call her late at night and have her sing me to sleep.

I miss her. She's gone and I miss her and all I want to do is scream about how much I miss her and how much I love her but I can't, I can't.

I take a shower, come back and crawl into bed, and scream

into my pillow until my throat is raw and I can finally, finally fall asleep.

When I wake up, that photo of us is still there, the last thing open on my phone, that comment waiting for me.

I say nothing.

THREE DAYS G O N E.

Maggie's funeral is today.

It's the only thing I can think as I go through school, sit in class.

She is going to be placed in a coffin shell and lowered into the ground and never, ever come back. The girl I loved, the girl I thought I had a future with, the girl who made me want to be a better, braver version of myself. Maggie is gone and I will never hear her laugh again or hold her while she falls asleep, my arm going numb under her weight but I would never dare move it and wake her up—

"Corinne?"

I blink. Everyone else has left chemistry, and I'm still sitting here with my textbook open, not even looking at the page.

Haley is frowning down at me. "You spaced out."

"Yeah, I got that," I say, and shut my book and stuff it in my bag.

"You weren't at practice yesterday," she says.

"I know."

She frowns at me. For a second I think she's going to ask me if I'm okay, or something like that, but Haley isn't the type for sympathy or nice feelings. She says what she thinks and who cares how it makes anyone else feel.

Sometimes I wish I could be like that.

"Are you coming today?" she asks.

"I—probably not, I'm going through some family stuff. Julia knows, though," I say. Haley raises an eyebrow but doesn't say anything else.

I begin to feel sick around lunch.

Maggie's dead, Maggie's gone, Maggie died—

I'm not going to make it through the rest of my classes, not going to be able to sit here while everyone else laughs and carries on like nothing has happened, like the world hasn't shifted.

I head to my locker, grab my books and my keys.

Julia's coming toward me, waving her arms, trying to get my attention, but if she talks to me I'll scream.

I run away before she can find me.

Our house is empty; Dad's at work and Bysshe is asleep in a patch of sun. I throw my bags by the door, sink against it.

I'm going to have to go to the funeral. I'm going to have to go in—I can't skip, not after the wake, not after what Dylan said.

How am I going to get through this? How am I supposed to go on without her, like nothing's happened, like she isn't gone?

If I go, it'll be final, but if I don't . . .

I can't think about it.

My phone buzzes.

You ok? Didnt see you at lunch.

Trent. My ex. Sort-of friend.

Not like we're close enough that I'd tell him about Maggie. I don't know how he'd feel, me dating a girl just months after I broke up with him.

But it's sweet that he still checks in, that he cares.

Yeah. Stomach bug. Thanks for checking, I type back, and flop down on the couch.

My phone buzzes again a minute later, but I just leave it on the coffee table and close my eyes.

I think I sleep.

Around four, my phone buzzes again, and I pick it up and half-heartedly think about just texting Trent everything.

But it's not him. It's some unknown number asking if I'm going to the funeral and if I want company, and I remember—

Elissa.

Part of me wants to text and tell her to fuck off, because I'm still angry that Maggie didn't tell me about her, but the other, stronger part just doesn't want to do this alone.

Before I can talk myself out of it, I text her and say yes, I'd like a ride, and can she pick me up; I live off Kirkland Road.

She replies a minute later.

Sure. I know where you're at. See you then.

My dead girlfriend's ex is driving me to her funeral.

This is so fucked up.

Elissa pulls up to my house right at 4:45, in the same blue pickup she was driving yesterday. It's strange to see her behind the wheel. Most of the people who drive pickups here are the boys at my high school, revving their engines in the parking lot like some show of whose dick is bigger.

I jog down to meet her, tug on the hem of my navy dress, hair pulled back. I almost put my cross-country jacket on but decided against it at the last minute. I already feel like I don't belong at Maggie's funeral, and calling attention to it by wearing the jacket would have just made it so much worse. So I settled on a plain navy one that's a little too small and a slightly different color than the dress, but it's still warm.

I hop up into Elissa's truck and buckle my seat belt as she pulls out of my driveway.

"You look nice," she says, still staring straight ahead. I glance over at her. She's in another dark button-down and black slacks. She looks handsome.

That thought feels like a betrayal—thinking another girl looks handsome, let alone my girlfriend's ex, let alone the ex who's driving me to that same girlfriend's funeral.

Maggie dated her. Maggie dated her and didn't tell me about

it, never discussed who she'd dated. Never mentioned her once. And here she is, and she might be grieving just like I am but I wouldn't know because until two days ago I had no idea who she was and Maggie never mentioned her why did Maggie never mention her?

Because that's the thing—I don't remember her mentioning Elissa. Not the name exactly, though maybe she mentioned an ex at some point. Truth be told, I didn't pay attention, didn't want to think about it, about Maggie with other girls.

Because what if she was comparing me to them? Especially if she'd been with girls who were already out, girls who knew what they wanted, girls who had known they liked girls since the age of eleven, and here I was, a fraud at sixteen who'd never even *kissed* a girl.

She never mentioned her but I never asked, and maybe I should have.

No. I know I should have.

Elissa's car rolls to a stop at a light, the only one in our town.

We pass by a pizza joint with an arcade in the back, and I turn my head so I don't have to see it. Julia took me there right when I moved, and we passed the time eating pizza and I showed her how good I was at Ms. Pac-Man, how I'd had the pattern memorized since I was a kid and Mom and I played while we waited at the movies, quarters shoved into our pockets.

I was going to take Maggie there, show it to her. But I was

always afraid of running into someone we knew.

Anyway. It's too late now.

"How are you doing?" Elissa asks, and it takes a minute to register again she's talking to me, I'm so lost in my own thoughts.

"I'm . . . I don't know," I say, and it's the first time since I found out about Maggie that I've said something honest, surprising myself.

But Elissa gets it. As much as I resent Dylan for forcing us together, that's not her fault.

She nods. "Yeah. I—yeah. I get that. It's weird—to think that she's gone, you know?"

I do know, but I can't say that, can't force the words out of my mouth. So I ask her something different.

"How did you meet Maggie?"

"High school. I was on tech when they did *Thoroughly Modern Millie* two years ago. Only show I ever did," she says. "Maggie was our stage manager. Sophomore, but she'd mess you up if you talked backstage. We met when I went outside for a smoke break during dress rehearsal and she came outside to complain about the actors. We hit it off, started dating," she says as she fishes around in her pocket for a cigarette. "You mind if I smoke in here?"

"It's your car."

"That's not what I asked."

"Yes," I say. "I mind."

She begins drumming her fingers on the steering wheel. "I quit, you know. I mean . . . Maggie wanted me to quit so I quit, but when I found out she died, I just . . . Old habits die hard."

I flinch, and she looks over at me.

"Shit. Sorry. That came out wrong."

"How'd you find out?" I ask quietly.

"Dylan called me, said he figured I'd hear it from someone at school sooner or later so he wanted to go ahead and tell me."

"Dylan called you?" I can't even keep the jealousy out of my voice.

She looks over at me. "Yeah."

The sadness that was building in my chest quickly turns to rage. "Unbelievable."

"What?"

"*You* get a call, and I have to figure it out from some girls in the locker room?" My voice grows shrill, like it always does when I'm angry, and it just makes me angrier, but I can't stop. "We'd been together for almost a *year* and no one thinks to do anything about it, no one thinks to call or tell me?" I take a deep, shuddering breath, ball my hands into fists, and dig my nails into my palms. I can feel tears pricking at the backs of my eyes, but I will be damned if I cry now.

"I'm sorry Dylan didn't call you," Elissa says after a minute. "He should have. That was shitty."

"Yeah." I sniff. "It was." I open the console to root around for a napkin or a tissue, grab one that looks like it's been in there for a while, and blow my nose into it.

It's not Elissa's fault Dylan didn't tell me. But the fact that she knew and I didn't, the fact that he didn't even think to call me, burns me up inside.

The car slows to a stop and I look up, crumple the tissue in my palm.

We're here.

The parking lot is packed with mourners, black-feathered crows come to gawk at the dead girl. Leesboro's cross-country team stands in a pack, all in their jackets. Next to them is a group of girls in colors too bright for a funeral—the drama department.

But with a start, I think, Maggie would have liked those colors. Maggie hated black. The drama department is doing more to honor her memory than I am.

Do I get to honor her memory anymore, though, if her brother didn't even call me to tell me she died?

"I don't want to go in," I say as Elissa pulls out of the parking lot and parks her truck on the street. "I don't want to do this."

She looks over at me.

"Suck it up, Corinne," she says, her voice raw. "You think you're the only one grieving? You think anyone here is going to notice you? Maggie would have wanted you here, okay?"

That hits me. Elissa must notice, because she looks away from me before she steps out of the truck. I stumble out, wobbling on heels that I never wear. For a split second I think I'm about to go down, fall on the pavement and just lie there in a crumpled heap for the entire service, but Elissa grips my arm and pulls me back up. I'm surprised by how strong she is.

"Jesus," I snap, brushing her off. "You're going to crush me."

She shrugs, but the look she gives me tells me she would rather have let me fall.

The church is packed. Elissa and I stand at the back, away from Maggie's family and from all the girls from her high school.

I think they can tell I don't belong. I think they can all tell. Girls can sense that. It's what we're trained for, some twisted survival mechanism.

Our backs are pressed against the wall of the church. In front of us is a sea of black, sniffing students and parents and teachers.

No one looks at the Baileys when they walk in, like their grief is contagious, like the people we love will die if we look at them or touch them.

I gather a piece of my dress in my fingers, play with it so I can give myself something to focus on as the pastor drones on about Maggie being in a better place and about it being her time. If he says something about God needing another angel or some bullshit like that, I will stand on a church pew and scream.

Maggie believed in all this. Maggie believed in God, she

prayed before meals and did youth group on Sundays, and I wanted to ask her—how? How could she hold on to that faith when so many other people in her church would have shunned her if they'd known about us? How could she believe in a God so many other people weaponized against her?

I will never have the chance to ask her.

The pastor stops talking, and there are murmurs as everyone in front of us reaches for hymnals, a collective clearing of throats and rustling of pages. Elissa shifts next to me. I'd forgotten she was there.

The piano starts up and the lump in my throat gets bigger because it's "How Great Thou Art," which was Maggie's favorite.

She made me go to church with her once and they'd sung it, and I'd stood and watched as she sang along even though she always said her voice was terrible.

It didn't mean to me what it did to her, but hearing it now nearly bowls me over, because in all these voices singing the chorus, hers isn't among them.

"Do you want to step outside?" Elissa whispers as the congregation moves to the second verse.

I shake my head. "I'll be fine."

"You sure?"

"Back off, Elissa," I snap, and she steps away from me, nearly running into another cross-country girl who turns to look at the two of us like we don't belong here.

I don't belong here. I don't belong with these grieving girls, girls who get a claim to Maggie while all I got were stolen moments and kisses in her basement.

But I think of what Elissa said, how Maggie would have wanted me here, and I can't make myself leave.

I don't know how I make it through the funeral. I hold pieces of myself together by leaning on the back wall and closing my eyes, thinking about Maggie, about her smile, about how she would have cracked a joke to get me to laugh, to get all of us to laugh, because she couldn't stand to see anyone cry.

I'm going to make it through this, I'm going to be okay—

And then Dylan stands up. His face is red even though he isn't crying, his grief reverberating throughout the room.

If Maggie were here, she would comfort him. They were close, especially since they were only two years apart, and if she were here—

But she isn't. She isn't here, and the rest of us are, and we are the ones who have to go on without her even though we can't and it just isn't *fair*.

Dylan clears his throat, and through a gap in the crowd I can see—

He has his hand on the coffin. Her coffin. And he's leaning on it like I am on this wall, other hand trembling as he holds a piece of paper out in front of him.

He clears his throat again, and someone breaks out into loud sobs before he's even started. For a second I think it's one of the drama girls, but no—it's Mrs. Bailey. Collapsed onto her husband's shoulder, body shaking.

"Maggie," Dylan begins, and him saying her name, the sound of it in his mouth, somehow makes this more real, and I grip Elissa's arm to keep from falling again. "Maggie . . . my sister . . . she was great. She was a winner, and I think everyone in here knows that—she would do whatever it took to win."

He says it with pride, with sadness, but the cross-country girls in front of me shoot glances at each other.

Maggie was competitive, if you were being nice. If you weren't, she was sometimes a bitch, with a perfectionist streak not only for herself but for everyone around her.

But no one here is going to say that. They probably won't ever again. Death does that to teenage girls—makes martyrs out of them, perfect angels with white wings and halos that don't quite fit.

"She was so driven," Dylan says, "And she really wanted to use that, to help people—especially kids, she was really good with kids. Her favorite thing to do on Sunday evenings was to volunteer with the youth group. She was . . ." His voice cracks, which brings on a fresh round of sobs from Mrs. Bailey. "She wanted to be a teacher."

Something inside me cracks. I didn't know that. I didn't

know Maggie wanted to teach; we never talked about it. She never told me.

She didn't tell me about teaching, about Elissa. I knew so many things about her but not these things, and I think—God, did I even know her at all?

No. I did. I have to cling to that. I did know her; I knew so much about her because I loved her, because if I admit I didn't know her and she isn't here anymore to tell me—

I can't deal with that.

I turn my attention back to Dylan. He's lowered his paper, his face as red as his hair, and then he starts crying. Not the open sobs of Mrs. Bailey, but tears are streaming down his face, no effort to hide it. A sense of unease fills the air, uncomfortable shifting because Dylan is openly crying, leaning on his sister's coffin to support himself. Unease because God forbid a boy—man, I guess, since he's in college—cry so openly even though his sister has died. Better he keep it in, bottle it up, so the rest of us don't have to be uncomfortable.

But Dylan is standing in front of us, and he is crying.

After a minute some of his college friends get up and lead him back to his seat, where he sits next to his parents, their heads bowed, arms around each other.

I can't do this. I can't stand here and watch them carry her coffin out, as her family walks out and everyone shuffles behind them whispering, I can't.

I mumble something to Elissa about needing to get some air. She wordlessly presses her keys into my palm in understanding, and as soon as I push my way out of the church I run to the truck and lock myself inside.

Elissa stands around in the parking lot for a good while after everyone has walked out, talking with a few other mourners who look about her age. Some of the theater girls come up to her and hug her.

Do they know? Do they know who she was to Maggie?

I watch her. The way she deftly lights a cigarette, the way one of the girls touches her arm and she tips her head back and laughs. I can see why Maggie liked her and I hate that I can.

What are they talking about, these girls? What are they saying that I don't know?

And that question comes back to me again, how much did I really know about Maggie?

Do I even deserve to grieve her?

Elissa gets back in her truck a few minutes later, smelling like cigarettes and the perfume of one of the drama girls. She starts her car but doesn't move it out of park, just sitting there for a minute.

She reaches over and touches my hand, softly, like she's not sure if she should. "Hey," she asks. "Do you . . . do you want to go to the gravesite?"

"I . . . do you?"

She shrugs, blows air out. "Not . . . not really? Because if I see them put her in the ground—" she stops. "I just . . . I can't do it, you know?"

Her words echo exactly what I've been feeling and thinking, and for a minute I don't feel so empty because here is a girl who gets it, who understands what I'm going through. I want to reach out to her, but every time I can feel myself trying, I think—

Why didn't Maggie tell me about you?

"I don't want to either," I say, and she nods.

Maggie is going to be buried in a cemetery next to the park she used to play at as a kid. Where she fell from the slide and lost a tooth, where Mariah Davis was mean to her in the sandbox and made her cry. She is going to be buried there and her ex-girlfriend and I will not be there to see them lower her into the ground.

And then . . . that will be it.

Elissa starts her truck. "If we're not going . . . what do you want to do?"

And the thought that I still don't have anything tangible from her, not really, hits me again.

"I want her stuff," I say suddenly, blurting the words out of my mouth. "Her—her running stuff."

"Where is it?"

"Her house," I say.

Elissa sighs, but she doesn't move the car out of park. "Corinne . . ."

"I need it, Elissa," I say. "I—we weren't out, and running is what we had in common and I *need*—"

"I get it," she says, cutting me off. Then, "Why weren't you out?"

Panic rises in my throat at her question, panic and something else, something sour.

I think it's guilt.

I *know* it's guilt.

"Because—because—" I say, but I can't get the words out. "We . . . we weren't ready."

Elissa frowns at that, but she doesn't say anything else about it.

"If you want her stuff, we're going to have to wait for Dylan," she says. "Or her parents. You can't just walk into their house."

"I know," I say. Then, "Could you come with me? I mean I know you'll have to drive me, but I mean—could you come in with me? I don't want to be alone."

For a split second, her hands tighten on the steering wheel and I think she's about to cry. Then she exhales, long and slow.

"Yes," she says. "I can do that."

"Are . . . are you okay?" I ask, because it occurs to me then, she knew Maggie as well as I do—did. She dated her, too.

She lost her, too.

"Funerals just kinda freak me out a bit," Elissa says, running her fingers through her curls. "I'll be okay."

"Okay," I say. "You . . . you really don't have to go with me if you don't want."

"No," she says. "I should." She takes another deep breath. "I'll go ask Dylan, okay? He's probably going to the gravesite, so we'll have to wait, but if he's okay with it, we'll go."

"Okay," I say, and wait as she gets out of the car, leaving it running.

Her question comes back to me as she shuts the door.

Why weren't you out?

I know the answer to that question, but I can't think about it, not now.

I start to cry again. Maggie's gone and we weren't out and now neither of us will get that chance, because she isn't here and I'm too scared to do it without her.

She deserved better than me.

Elissa comes back five minutes later, and I know she smoked, because she smells even more like cigarettes.

"Dylan said we could meet him there," she says. "His parents are staying with his aunt for the night since it's too hard for them to be home, so. I think that's where they're dropping all the food off, too, so we shouldn't run into anyone."

"Okay," I say. Elissa puts the car into gear and starts to drive. I keep my gaze down at my lap, resist the urge to pull out my phone.

"So," Elissa says as we turn on a back road, "Um. How's school?"

"You sound like my dad."

She barks a laugh. "Sorry. We don't have to talk if you don't want."

"No, the distraction is nice," I say. "Um. It's okay. Cross-country's going to eat up a lot of my time. Coach wants us to place for State this year if we can, since some of the better runners are graduating."

"How does that work?"

"Kinda like you'd expect. We've gotta be fast enough as a team to qualify for Regionals, then Coach submits seven of us for that, then if the team places in the top twenty-five percent, we go to State."

"Have you been before?"

"No," I say. "I'm not that good. Maggie . . . Maggie was, though. But she didn't make it either last year—her team almost qualified, but not quite."

She was going to this year, though. We'd talked about it over the summer. She was going to push herself even harder to make it to State.

She wanted me there with her.

"That doesn't surprise me," Elissa says. "She always was a perfectionist."

To my surprise, I laugh. Because she's right. Because she knows that part of Maggie.

"What about you?" I ask. "I guess you're in school, right?"

"Yeah. I'm studying computer science, but I'm doing community college first. My dad's a chemical engineer, so . . . yeah. He wasn't super happy about Wake Tech but if I can get my basics out of the way it's cheaper for us and it's easier for me to get into a four-year program in the future." She looks over at me. "What about you? What do you want to do when you graduate?"

"You make me feel really young," I say, surprising myself.

"I'm only two years older than you."

"Yeah, but . . . never mind," I say. "And I don't know. I thought about doing something with chemistry, maybe."

Elissa looks surprised. "Really?"

"Well, yeah, why not?"

Though I know why not; I know what she's going to say before she even says it.

"You don't look like the type."

I look down. At my navy dress from J. Crew my mom bought out of guilt for missing my seventeenth birthday, my chipped pink nail polish, the blond hair pulled back from my face. My hands, perfectly white-girl tanned from cross-country.

"What do I look like, then?" I ask.

Elissa shakes her head. "Forget it. I shouldn't have—forget it."

"Elissa—"

She holds up a hand, and we're silent until she pulls into Maggie's driveway.

Automatically I look for her car, but it isn't here. The image of it wrapped around a tree from the news two nights ago flashes through my mind—

Oh. God. What was it like? I barely watched the news, didn't want to see, but suddenly the only thing I can imagine is her final moments, her car swerving into a tree, phone and purse and Maggie all flying toward the windshield—

I can't think that.

I'm about to say something about it when Dylan's car pulls up and I'm saved from opening my mouth. The three of us get out of our cars at the same time, congregating on the sidewalk in front of the house like we're scared to go inside.

Dylan looks at me. "Why do you want her stuff, Corinne?" he asks, and his voice has an edge to it I wasn't expecting.

"I . . ." I falter. "Because—because I want something physical of hers and running is what we had together . . ."

He sighs. Stands there, staring at me.

"Let her have it, Dylan," Elissa says, surprising me. Dylan glances over at her, and she shrugs. "What else are you going to do with it?"

He chews on his bottom lip. "I . . . okay." He pulls a key out of his pocket and unlocks the door.

Her house smells the same. Not like her, not quite, but cozy in that way other people's houses smell.

"Come on," Dylan says, and starts up the stairs, Elissa and me trailing behind him.

I stop as we're going up the stairs, can't help but look at the photos of Dylan and Maggie that line the walls—them at Disney World when she was a kid, last year in New York in front of the marquee for *Phantom of the Opera*, Maggie grinning ear to ear. The resemblance between the two of them is uncanny in photographs, and I hate that's all that's going to be left of her, these photos and whatever runs through Dylan's head each time he looks in the mirror.

The three of us stop in front of her room. The door is closed, but other than that, everything looks the same. Like we're all just waiting for her to come back.

"Her running stuff is still in the closet," Dylan says. "I . . . you can do this without me." Elissa reaches out a hand and touches Dylan on the shoulder, but he shrugs her off. "I'll be downstairs," he says shortly, and then disappears. She looks over at me.

"You ready?"

"No," I say. But I'm the one who wanted to do this.

"Do you want me to go in with you?"

"I . . . in a minute," I say, and she nods.

"I'll wait out here."

I take a breath and steel myself, then push the door open.

It looks the same. I don't know why I thought it wouldn't. The walls are still lavender. I'd tease her about that, because it was such an Easter-bonnet little-girl color, but she didn't mind. I'd tease her about the horse posters shoved under her bed, too, the Twilight books proudly hanging out on her bookshelf, because she was so typical, because she was such a *girl*.

The only thing that's changed is the bulletin board above her headboard. What was covered with brochures from Oklahoma State, Florida State, is now covered with a recruiting letter from Villanova.

Seeing that letter makes my chest burn. Not from jealousy, not from the fact that Maggie was being recruited by Division I colleges when I'm not, but from the fact that she wanted to travel all the way to Pennsylvania for college, that she'd made up her mind without me.

I was so scared of her leaving me, and now she has.

Her bed isn't made. I try not to look at it, try not to think of the hours we spent kissing in that bed when no one was home or the warmth of her back against mine when I slept over, or or or—

God, I can't do this.

I turn my back to the bed, press my hand over my mouth so Elissa can't hear me crying. It takes a minute before I can go into the closet and look at the box of her running stuff. It's an old cardboard box, one that maybe held a Christmas present or some childhood toys in the attic and now all it holds is what's left of Maggie's running.

I close my eyes and open the box, just feeling around her running clothes and her spikes and Leesboro's cross-country handbook. And then my fingers brush across something else, and I know immediately what it is.

I pull it out, open my eyes. In my hand is the lime-green scrunchie she wore every meet. There are a few strands of her hair still caught in it and I try not to think about that as I slip it around my wrist.

It smells like her. I don't want it to but it does, more than her room does, more than anything in this box, this scrunchie smells like her shampoo and her perfume and race days and us.

She thought it was lucky. She swore it was, swore she performed better when she wore it.

I slip it around my wrist. I don't feel any luckier. Maggie's gone and I'm standing in her room with a box of her running stuff and all I feel is angry and sad and lost.

"Corinne?"

I look up. Elissa is standing in the doorway, concern all over her face.

"Is that it?" she asks, and I wipe at my eyes.

"Yeah."

She comes over and bends down beside me, settling herself on the floor. She doesn't go for the box. Instead, she reaches in the closet and pulls out a stack of papers—playbills from shows—and begins flipping through them.

"There was one Halloween we dated where she made me dress up like the Phantom, and she was Christine," Elissa says. "I think I still have the mask in a closet somewhere."

"God, she loved that musical," I say. "But she hated the movie."

"Oh, you couldn't get her started on it, she'd go on about it for ages," Elissa says, and she laughs. "Did she make you watch the filmed live version, though?"

"Only like, five times," I say. "I never told her I slept through one of them."

"Same," Elissa says, and she catches my eye. "It's nice," she says. "Being able to talk about her with you. With—with someone who really knew her."

I want to agree with her. I really, really do. But then I remember that Maggie never told me about her, Elissa knew who I was but Maggie never told me and she knew all these things and I—

I don't say anything. I clutch the box to my chest, eager to get out of her room suddenly, her house, because I don't know who I'm angrier at, Maggie for never telling me or myself for never asking.

SEVEN MONTHS BEFORE.

I list the boys on my fingers, my head on her stomach, her hands in my hair.

"There was Bryce Hinson, back in Colorado," I say. "Though he was in middle school, so he didn't really count. Jeremy Hayes, when I first moved here. And Trent Moore, a few months ago."

"Why'd you break it off with Trent?" she asks.

I shrug. "He wanted me to meet his parents and come over for Thanksgiving, and I just—I couldn't. I liked him but I couldn't. So I ended it."

She nods. "Was it different with them?"

"Yes and no. I mean . . ." I trail off.

I didn't have to hide it with the boys, but now doesn't feel like the time to bring that up.

I should ask who she dated, but I don't want to know. Don't want to think about other girls before me, what she was like with them.

She sits up and pulls me to her, kisses me, and soon I forget about Trent, Bryce, Jeremy, everyone in our past who isn't her.

FOUR DAYS G O N E.

I wake up on Friday groggy and delirious, reach for my phone, forgetting for a second—

And then I remember. The wake. The funeral. Elissa, riding in her truck, the fact that everyone seemed to know her.

I scroll through Instagram. There are twenty new comments on Maggie's last post.

I read every. single. one of them.

you would have loved the funeral. such a beautiful service and they played ur song

The youth group really misses you. We're helping out at the harvest fest next week and it's weird planning it without you.

Practice is soooooo weird without you girl.

Looking at these hurts, but I can't stop myself. I switch back to her Facebook, but there's only one new post on her wall, one from Mrs. Bailey. I almost don't read it, almost don't look because it feels so private, her grief on display.

Your father and I miss you so much. He's having a really hard time with it. I am too. So many people came out yesterday to celebrate your life. You were so loved, sweetheart. So loved by everyone, especially us.

I exit the app, turn my phone off and place it on my nightstand, curling up on my side in bed. I feel so selfish for mourning when Mrs. Bailey is really hurting, selfish for thinking of myself rather than Maggie's family.

But I lost her, too.

I push myself out of bed, stretch on the floor, and change— skinny jeans, knee-high boots I saved up for months working at the ice cream shop to buy because all the girls on the cross-country team wear them. They don't quite fit, but that doesn't matter. They make me look like I belong, and that is what's important.

When we moved here the summer after my freshman year, I made a promise to myself in the back of the car as we crossed the border into North Carolina—no matter what it took, no matter how it made me feel, I would look like I belonged here. I would look like I was happy, be one of those perfect, shining girls everyone wants to be.

Even then the distance between my parents was growing, no matter how much they tried to hide it from me. So I decided: if their marriage couldn't be perfect, then I had to be, to make things as easy as possible on them.

And then they got divorced anyway. But Dad got the majority of the custody, and I know he doesn't know what to do with a teenage girl, so it's better for him if I just—keep on pretending. Keep on lying.

I'm good at that.

There's a knock on my door before Dad pokes his head in, right when I'm pulling a shirt on over my sports bra.

"Knocking means you're going to wait for me to say come in before you just open the door," I say.

He rolls his eyes, looks around my messy room. "Why aren't you packed yet?"

"Packed?"

"It's your mother's turn this weekend, remember?" he says.

Shit. Mom. Right.

My mother gets visitation rights two weekends out of every month. It would've been more, but the DUIs on her record didn't exactly endear her to the county judge, and the fact she walked in the morning of the custody hearing wobbly and smelling of booze just sealed the deal.

"I don't want to go," I say. "She'll just be drunk the whole weekend."

My dad's face contorts like he's smelled something awful. "Corey, be nice. She's trying."

I resist the urge to recite back to him exactly how many drinks it takes to get her drunk, whether that's in beer or wine or cocktails. Doesn't matter, I know them all by heart.

"Okay, but I'm packing a Breathalyzer," I joke, and he frowns.

"You have a meet tomorrow, right?" he says, abruptly changing the subject, rubbing the back of his neck, the actual conversations we will never have about my mother's alcoholism still making him uncomfortable. We don't mention it unless it's as a joke, something easy to laugh off and ignore.

"Yup," I say. "Against Greenwood."

"Do you want me to go?"

"No need," I say, turning and stuffing my spikes and an Ursula K. Le Guin novel into my duffel bag. "We'll crush them anyway, no need for you to drive out to see that."

"I like watching you win."

I smile. I know my dad doesn't understand the hype around running—he's never been an athlete—but the fact that he cares, that he tries, more than makes up for it.

A small part of me whispers he likes watching me win because it means I'll get out of here like he wants me to, but I stuff it down. Mom's never shown up to a meet once, so in the game of "which parent cares more," he's the one who's winning.

Maggie's parents went to every single meet. Dylan would, too, she told me, before he left for college.

Guess they don't have to go anymore, since they don't have anyone to watch, and it would be awkward if they still showed up now that their daughter is dead. Some people would think it's pathetic, even, probably. We only tolerate grief down here for so long before you're just expected to get over it.

"Not today, Dad," I say. "Save it for the bigger races."

He nods. "Can't wait to see you at those bigger races, Corey. I'll sit right next to the scouts and tell them to watch out for you."

"Dad," I say, but fear at his words twists inside me. "You wouldn't."

"Don't underestimate me," he says, and winks. Before I can reply, ask if he's joking though I know he's not, Bysshe comes in and tangles himself around Dad's ankles. Dad scoops him up and kisses the top of his head, then heads down the stairs.

"Don't be late for school," he shouts, and with that, he's gone.

ONE YEAR BEFORE.

She's already inside when I walk up to the coffee shop, sitting by the window. She's got on a cute purple top, forest-green coat draped over her chair, and earrings, things I've never seen her in on race days.

My heart beats even faster.

But this is just two girls in a coffee shop, two high school girls who want to get to know each other better. I have a boyfriend, and I don't feel that way about her, and this doesn't mean anything.

There's a ding when I walk in, and she looks up immediately, excitement clear on her face even though we're just here for coffee.

But the way she looks at me feels different. "Hi!" she says, pushing back from her chair, and before I know it she's hugging me. She smells like honeysuckle, Southern summers, and my hands shake when I press them against her back.

. . .

"Hi," I say, and she beams at me. I sit across from her, take my coat off and hang it on the back of the chair.

My phone buzzes when I do. It's Trent, wanting to know if I'm coming over tomorrow after the game.

I put it back in my pocket. Talking to him when I'm out with this girl feels wrong. Rude.

"Who's that?" she asks.

"My boyfriend," I say.

"Oh," she says, and when I glance at her, do I see a flicker of disappointment across her face?

"We're not serious," I say. "I mean, I guess we're getting there—he wants me to come over for Thanksgiving and meet his parents and everything. Even his grandma."

"Damn," she says. "Grandma. That is serious."

I laugh, but there's a twinge of fear in my gut. "I guess." I shrug, watch as she takes a sip of her coffee. "Do you have a boyfriend?"

I don't know why I'm asking. To make conversation, I guess.

She ducks her head and smiles. "No," she says. "I don't."

There's something to that but I don't think about what.

We talk. About running, about moving, the difference between Colorado and North Carolina winters. About her brother, away in college. About how it's almost like he has to live up to her expectations rather than the other way around, even though he's older. I tell her about having divorced parents, spending weekends splitting yourself in two. Taking sides even when you shouldn't, subconsciously.

We talk and I get to know her better and I think, we could be friends. Even though we're competing against each other at every race. We could be actual friends.

She hugs me again when we leave, and electricity zings through me at her touch.

Do you have a boyfriend?

No. I don't.

Why does that thought fill me with something I can't explain?

I think about her the entire ride home.

FOUR DAYS G O N E.

Dad's words echo in my head as I sit down at lunch.

He's never made it a secret that he expects running is how I'm going to get out of North Carolina, go to a big college, and never look back. He's counting on a scholarship, several scholarships, so I can escape student loans like the ones he's still paying off.

He wants me to be better this year—at running. He's said so a few times, because the better I am, the better my chances of getting out of here.

Sometimes I think about it—getting out of this town, this state, but I can't picture it. Can't picture any sort of future for myself outside of what's immediately in front of me, even though I know I should.

Maggie could, though. She could picture this whole grand future for us, and it was easy to let her. She tried to get me to train with her this summer so that when the fall season started, we'd be on almost equal ground.

But she was always better than me. No amount of training was going to change that.

Still. I would try. Because that is what perfect girls do.

TrentandChrisandJulia are already sitting at our shared table, swapping food and stories, when I walk up. Julia scoots over to make room for me on the bench next to her.

Julia runs because she loves it; you can see it in how she performs. Chris is the same way. And Trent? Everything is easy for Trent. Football, classes, dating, doesn't matter. Everything comes easy to him, and sometimes I hate him for it.

Trent was the first one to invite me to sit with them. I'd met Julia when she told me to try out for cross-country, but we didn't become close friends until the season started. I'd entered the caf my second day with nowhere to sit, trying to figure it out because there wasn't so much a hierarchy as pockets of people who'd known each other since kindergarten, and here I was, completely new and not understanding anything.

And I saw Julia, but her back was to me, and then Trent was waving me over with that gleaming golden-boy smile, and I thought, okay, here is what shining perfect girls do, they sit with hot boys who must be athletes.

It was more than that, though—Trent made me feel welcome. I sat down at the table and he asked what I'd brought, and he cracked a joke and made me laugh, and before I knew it lunch was over. Before we even started dating, he was like that.

Going out of his way to make anyone feel welcome.

Without a word, Trent passes me a container filled with something, and as soon as I open the lid I can tell it's his grandma's homemade baklava.

"Thanks," I say, and he nods. I set it next to my tray of cafeteria food, poke at a glob of mashed potatoes with my fork.

"They're worse than normal," Chris says, eyeing them and grinning at me. "You shouldn't risk it."

"Your plate is clean," I say.

"I didn't say anything about not risking my own life," he says, and I laugh and pass my plate over to him. I like Chris. Like his wide smile, like how kindly he treats Julia.

"Take them. I'm not hungry."

"Are you sick?" Julia asks.

"PMS," I say, and it's true but not really. "Sorry."

Trent makes a face. "Can we not? We're eating."

Julia looks at him. "Really? It's not like she mentioned, I dunno, actively *bleeding*—"

Trent covers his ears. Actually covers them like a child. "That's fucking gross, Recinos."

"Grosser than any of your locker room talk?" Julia asks, an edge to her voice. She looks at me, waiting for me to back her up.

I should say something.

Should.

Should.

But the moment passes and we go back to eating. I make eye contact with Chris, who, I notice, isn't actually eating the mashed potatoes.

Trent is the first one to break the silence. "How is the season going for y'all?" he asks, looking eager to change the subject.

"It's okay," Julia says, shrugging. "Not as good as last year. We've got a few runners who might make it to Regionals, and maybe, like, one or two who'll make it to State."

She means herself and Haley. I'm not good enough for State; Coach Reynolds says I could be if my heart was in it more, but it never has been.

But I think back to what my dad said this morning, what Maggie wanted, and I wonder if my heart should be in it, if I should be trying harder this year, trying to run faster get a scholarship get out of here, rather than just being good enough. Rather than just keeping my head down and not making waves, one foot in front of the other.

"Y'all started getting recruiting calls yet?" Chris asks.

Julia's cheeks turn pink. "A few. But you knew that."

He grins at her and reaches across the table, twining his dark brown fingers with her lighter ones. There's real pride in Chris's face when Julia talks about how good she's doing. She knows she's a good athlete. He does, too. They've been together since freshman year and we all swear they're going to be professional athletes and get married someday, though leaving North Carolina is not part of that future. No one ever leaves here unless it's by a miracle, even if they probably could, because we all just feel stuck. Chris will play football for the Carolina Panthers or some college team, Duke maybe, and Julia will go to a local arts school if she doesn't get a scholarship for running. They are the golden couple of our high school, and it'd be easy to hate them for it if they weren't so damn supportive of each other.

"Has anyone called you yet, Corinne?" Trent asks, mouth full of fried chicken.

I shrug. "A few places," I lie, because this is what I should say, this is how it should be happening.

No one has called me. If I were a different girl I would be worried about this, and maybe I should be, especially now that Maggie's gone . . .

It's hard to think of a future without her in it.

"Maybe Aldersgate will call," I say, trying to sound casual.

"Aldersgate?" Trent says. "But they're such a small school."

I don't say that Aldersgate is where my father went, where I'll probably go, where I'd tried to convince Maggie to join me so we could be together even though we both knew she was destined for bigger things. I don't say I'm looking at it because it's a small private college and I could get a pretty substantial scholarship, and my mom's mostly unemployed and my parents are divorced and Dad's job as an IT guy doesn't make much, that college wasn't even on the table for me until I started running. But Trent doesn't need to know that.

"Where else have you been recruited?" I ask, not just Julia

but Trent and Chris, too, since schools have been scouting them about the same time they've been scouting us.

"Oklahoma, Clemson, Duke," Julia says, at the same time that Trent and Chris say, "Chapel Hill."

"Oh God," I say. Because that was the first thing I learned when I moved down here, that people will put aside whatever differences you have as long as you root for the right shade of blue come football or basketball season.

Dad pulls for East Carolina, out of spite and because he knows nothing about football. I root for whoever's winning.

"I'll still love you even if you go to the wrong school," Chris says to Julia, and he leans across the table and kisses her on the cheek while Trent and I look on awkwardly.

I stare down at my cafeteria tray. Maggie and I talked about school a few times, about the possibility of us ending up in the same place, somewhere big we could be out and no one cared.

But now she's gone and I have to make all my decisions alone.

THREE MONTHS BEFORE.

We're snuggled under the covers on her bed, in just T-shirts and underwear even though it's cold in her room, the air-conditioning blasting. Her parents are out at a dinner party; Dad thinks I'm with Julia.

"How was your visit?" I ask, kissing her. She had an official visit at Clemson this past weekend, even though senior year hasn't even started. It's the first we've spoken of it since we got back, not because we spent too much time kissing (we did) but because I haven't wanted to hear that she loved it.

"It was good," she says. She moves, and my head falls back on the bed. I watch as she stands, pulls her bra on. I've always been amazed she can clasp it from the back; I have to twist mine around to the front to fasten it.

"Actually, it was great. I really liked it," she says, and she turns back around to face me. "Like, the team was good and the coach was really nice and I could see myself fitting in there."

"That's great," I say. Then, "Why'd you downplay it?"

She shrugs. "I'm just worried about how you'll react."

I push myself up in bed. "Seriously?"

"I just . . . I don't know, Corinne," she says, her brow knitted. "My times are better than yours, and I just—I don't want you to worry if we end up at different schools."

But she's the one who wants us to go to the same place. It's all she talks about, and I wonder if she's trying to reassure herself, or me.

"I mean . . . I don't want you to waste your potential because of me," I say, and I try to make it sound like a joke, but it doesn't, because she just frowns and turns away, and I lie back down in her bed.

She curls back up next to me after a minute.

"You could be really good, you know?" she says softly, her fingers tracing the dip of my collarbone. "I could train with you."

"Really?"

"Mm-hmm," she says sleepily, and kisses my cheek.

"I'd like that," I say.

And then it's like her energy comes back, because she rolls over, her eyes bright.

"You would?"

"Yeah," I say, smiling up at her. "I would."

"Then let's go!"

She leans in to kiss me, tantalizingly close, then pulls back, laughing, going to her closet and pulling her tennis shoes out of the box of her running stuff she keeps in there.

I sit up. "You're not serious," I say, but there's laughter in my voice because I know that she is, because that's just how she is—she sees something she wants, and she goes after it. She doesn't wait.

"I am!" She chucks a pair of socks at my head. "Come on, sleepy butt."

"I'd better be getting a reward for this when I get back," I grumble, moving so I'm sitting on the edge of the bed.

Maggie comes over to me then, in just her bra and shorts, the expression on her face a challenge.

"If you beat me," she says, moving so she's straddling me, "I promise it'll be worth your while."

Her face is inches from mine. I tilt mine up to hers, closer, close my eyes . . .

And then feel something wet on my nose.

"Did you just—did you just *lick* my nose?"

Her weight is gone, and I open my eyes to see her laughing.

"Oh, I'm totally going to get you for that," I say, standing up, and she sticks her tongue out at me.

"You're going to have to catch me first."

FOUR DAYS G O N E.

I pull up to my mother's, and the second I get out of the car her chihuahuas, Linda and Lovelace, start barking behind the screen door.

Leave it to my mother to name her dogs after a porn star.

Dry fall grass brushes against my ankles as I walk up the sidewalk to her front door. She hasn't had anyone mow since July, and now September's bringing that first cold wave that'll turn green patches of grass to brown, overgrown ones. Guess she figured since it would all die soon she didn't need anyone to care for it, but it looks terrible, and I wish I could tell her so.

She's outlined through the screen door, my mother, Linda barking at her heels. Even through the mesh I can see she's in a tank top and shorts and clutching a glass of something.

"Corey!" she says, her voice loud and grating. My mother is not from here, but she adopted the Southern accent faster than either Dad or I did. She thinks it makes her sound more trustworthy, more fun. I think it makes her sound like a woman who's trying too hard. "Oh, I've missed you so much, come inside."

Her long nails dig into my shoulder as she steers me into the kitchen. I can remember a time she wasn't like this, but it's hazy, like looking back through a dirty glass. I can remember when I was in middle school and we lived in Colorado and she only drank for fun and she smelled like soap, not whatever was in her glass.

We got along then, even more than me and Dad. Mom would indulge me in the girly things I love, taking me for manicures, or shopping, and we'd actually talk. I'd tell her about school, about boys, about what I was reading or who I wanted to be when I grew up.

But when she started drinking when I was in middle school, we stopped going anywhere. Not all at once, not at first, more of a gradual trickling off, until it was just normal for her to be curled up with a bottle and me to be upstairs with homework.

I stopped talking. She stopped listening. Moving to North Carolina just exacerbated the problem. When we moved, she barely brought any of her stuff with her, like she already had one foot out the door. Before I even started my junior year, she left, and Dad and I were on our own.

It's a wonder we stayed in the same state, let alone a few miles from each other. But Dad didn't want to uproot me from school and agreed it would be easier for me to visit Mom if we all lived in the same area, at least until I go to college. So even though I know Mom misses her old friends and her old life and our old house she can't go back, not yet.

Part of me wonders if she resents me for that.

I would, if I were her.

Lovelace jumps and claws at my legs, and I wince. Mom doesn't notice, instead making a half-hearted wave to get the dogs to stop yapping, which they don't.

"Do you want a drink?" she asks as I set my bag down by the kitchen table. "I've got Coke, though I could make you something if you want."

Two minutes and she's offering me alcohol. It's a new record.

"I'm fine," I say.

"Want to sit down here with me?" she asks. "I'm just watching *Law & Order: SVU* reruns. We used to love doing that."

I'm surprised she remembers. Back in Colorado we'd watch *Law & Order: SVU* every weekend, because it was always on. We'd take turns guessing who the bad guy was, or which season it was based on Benson's haircuts. Winner got to pick wherever we'd go to dinner for Sunday night.

I always won, but what I didn't tell her was I'd watch them when I came home from school, before she got home from work. I guess it was cheating, but I liked to win back then. I liked the three of us going out like a family and getting burgers at my favorite restaurant, and as long as I guessed who the correct bad guy was on *SVU*, then we would.

"Sure," I say, and follow her into the living room. We settle on her couch and she flips on the TV.

"Where's Brett?" I ask, referring to her current boyfriend, a pharmacist she met online.

"He's getting ready to go referee," she says. "He does high school football. He'll be at your school in a few weeks; you should go."

"I didn't know that," I say.

"Mm-hmm. You can stay up with me tonight and we can look for him on TV."

Her acrylic nails tap on her wine glass, and suddenly that's the last thing I want to do. I doubt she'll make it to eleven o'clock to see him on the local news, anyway.

"Actually, could we go out for dinner?" I pick at the afghan covering the couch. "Like we used to—if I guess the bad guy on this episode correctly, I get to pick?"

She blinks. "Oh. Um. Sure, I guess," she says.

"I mean, we don't have to."

"No. No, baby, we can do that," she says. One of the dogs jumps up and settles itself on her lap, and I lean over at the opposite end of the couch.

It's pointless, but I hold out hope that we will. That we'll go out together like we used to. That if I guess every episode correctly, things will go back to the way they were.

I get all three episodes right, and she has a glass for every single one of them. By the time dinner rolls around, she's asleep on the couch.

I eat a bowl of cereal alone in my room.

FIVE DAYS G O N E.

I'm at Greenwood Park by nine a.m., pulling into an empty lot that isn't really a lot, just a bunch of gravel where we all leave our cars. Mom was still asleep when I left, dishes piling up in the sink and Brett nowhere to be seen.

Like it matters. Like I care.

I catch Julia's eye as I jog up to the rest of our team, Maggie's lime-green scrunchie in my hair. I almost didn't put it on this morning. But I need a little luck today, need something to help me get through this race.

Julia notices it, flicks it. "This is cute. Where'd you get it? It's not your usual color."

I shrug. "Found it somewhere," I say, and she accepts that without question because why wouldn't she?

Coach Reynolds pulls us all into a pep talk, blowing into the ever-present red whistle around her neck. Haley asks her some question and she smiles at her when she answers. I used to want to be the best on the team just so Coach Reynolds would pull out that rare smile and use it on me.

I used to.

But then I became another girl, I found another girl, and Coach Reynolds's approval didn't matter so much to me anymore. I just wanted to run after Maggie.

I would have followed that girl to the ends of the earth.

But Maggie is gone, and I don't know what I want anymore.

I follow Julia and Haley and the rest of our team to the starting line where we try to carve out spots for ourselves among the other girls waiting.

I know I shouldn't, but I look around for my mother before I start running. I know she won't be there, and I know Dad won't be because I asked him not to come, but it doesn't stop me from looking every damn time I step up to the starting line.

I want to tell myself she's not a bad mother, that she's been there when it's mattered, but the lie tastes sour on my tongue even if I don't say it out loud.

The starting whistle goes off, and Julia darts ahead of me. She likes to get farther ahead, then pace herself before a burst of speed at the end; I just run steadily the entire time because unlike her and Haley, I don't feel that need to push myself.

I'm doing well for me; I'm gaining a fair bit of speed and passing some of the slower runners from Greenwood like I know I should be doing. I'm not the slowest runner, and Julia's let it slip to me before that she counts on me in these races against Greenwood because it looks bad if I'm unable to beat any of them. Now that I'm a senior, I suspect she counts on me even more. The two of us and Haley are the only seniors on the team, and Julia stresses to us so much how the younger girls look up to us.

I don't want anyone looking up to me, though.

I round a bend, feel the strength of my spikes hitting the ground, kicking up clay and spattering my shins. Running makes me feel strong, good, capable. It's one of the few things that does.

But I'm rounding the corner to the finish line and my teammates are across the line when I see something that makes me go cold.

It's her. Maggie. It's her ponytail swinging in front of me and taunting me and I push myself and I run harder and harder and harder because if I can just catch her then everything will be okay; the world will have righted itself again.

I run, I run, I run with everything I have in me and I don't even see the finish line and when I cross it my teammates are surrounding me and whooping about how proud they are and how they haven't seen me run like that for ages and Julia is screaming something in my ear and even Coach is looking at me like she's proud.

But I don't register them. They are screaming and cheering and I don't register a sound because I am still looking for Maggie.

TEN MONTHS BEFORE.

Thanksgiving is here. State is over. We didn't make it; didn't even make it to Regionals. I know Coach was disappointed, but there's always next year.

Maggie did. Regionals, but not State. I texted and consoled her.

I should be thankful for another year. Thankful Trent took our breakup well.

He invited me over for Thanksgiving with his family, his cousins, playing some game called cornhole in the front yard. And I just . . . couldn't. I couldn't see myself doing it, couldn't see myself being introduced to his parents, his grandma, their perfect happy family. So I let him down.

At least it wasn't at Christmas.

I ask Maggie what she's doing for Thanksgiving, over text. She replies her brother's coming home and they're driving down to Kinston to visit her grandparents, a full family affair.

What are you doing?

I'm staying home with my dad, most likely eating an already-cooked chicken from the grocery store. Even when we were a family back in Colorado, Thanksgiving was never a big deal.

Maybe it should've been. Maybe if we'd done more for Thanksgiving, things wouldn't be how they are now.

You're welcome to come over when we get back. There'll be pie left. :)

Pie sounds good.

I pause, my fingers over the screen. I haven't told her I broke up with Trent. Not yet.

I broke up with Trent.

There.

I am just a girl telling her friend she broke up with a boy. Then why does it feel so significant, so much more than it is?

You like her.

I don't want to think about that.

FIVE DAYS G O N E.

The entire team goes out for pasta after our race to celebrate. All the girls are thumping me on the back, beaming at me when we reach the restaurant, and for a second I want to bask in the glow of this, truly feeling like I belong, because it's hardly ever happened to me before. Even Haley is smiling at me, not scowling like normal.

But then I remember why I ran, why I pushed myself so hard, and anything good I just felt vanishes.

I escape to the bathroom after I order, washing my hands and trying not to think about Maggie. Then Julia comes in, taking the sink right next to me.

"You did good today," she says, and I can't even be mad at her for the surprise in her tone.

"Thanks."

"I know what I said at lunch yesterday, but are you considering trying for State this year?" Julia asks. "If you kept running like you ran this meet, you'd have a shot."

State. State was something Maggie wanted, curly hair and gold-medal dreams. She wanted to try for it this year, since she got to Regionals last year and no girl from Leesboro had ever made it farther than that. She wanted to be the first one to do it, and now she will never get that chance.

"I don't know," I say.

Julia shrugs. "It's your decision. But you're good enough to this year. You might actually beat Haley."

"Yeah," I say, giving her a smile I don't entirely feel.

I want to tell her. I really, really want to tell her. She was the first person I told about my parents getting a divorce; I held her hand while she told me her sister Marisol had been diagnosed with depression and was dropping out of college and moving back in with her family.

But if I start to tell her about Maggie now, I won't be able to stop, and how can I tell Julia now that Maggie is gone?

Julia frowns and shuts off the sink. "Listen, you wanna come over tonight? I know you're spending the weekend with your mom and I also know how much you hate that."

I'd love to spend the night with Julia, love to sit up and gossip with her like we used to before Maggie, before I started making excuses.

But I think of Julia's house, of the crowd and noise of her siblings. "How about you stay with me? You know my mom doesn't care. We'll rent a movie and eat a shit ton of popcorn and chocolate."

"Okay," Julia says, face brightening, and guilt twists my stomach a little more, because the last time I had a sleepover with Julia was six months ago.

She shoots me a grin and heads out the door, opening it with her hip, and I hear her voice float away as she leaves me behind, leaves me alone.

Hours later Julia and I are curled up on my full-size bed, her head on my shoulder, *The Princess Diaries* playing in the background. My room at my mom's house is still filled with boxes because I haven't bothered to unpack, since I'm only here for a few days at a time.

When she first got the house, Mom promised that we'd spend the weekend painting it, just the two of us. Dad even agreed I could go over to her house when I wasn't scheduled to, and I was so, so excited. We went to the hardware store and bought paint, a pretty peach color I'd always liked.

But that Saturday when Dad dropped me off, she was already halfway through a bottle, too sloppy to hold a paintbrush. We drove home and the cans of paint stayed under the sink in her kitchen. I guess they're still there.

I should paint. I'd even thought about calling Maggie and planning to over the summer, asking her to help.

But I never did. She made me feel understood, she got me, but that didn't mean I wanted her to meet my mom.

Julia chews her way through two packs of Twizzlers, both

the red and black ones. I tease her all the time for liking licorice, because I think it's disgusting. I've got a bag of Kit Kats and am crunching through them steadily.

"You excited about college visits?" Julia asks as Mia discovers she's princess of Genovia. Julia pulls her thick, dark brown hair back into a ponytail.

"I guess." I pick at a thread in my comforter, one Mom bought from Target the first night I stayed with her because she didn't have anything else in the house. "You?"

"Totally excited," she says, Twizzler hanging out of the end of her mouth. "I'm even looking at Clemson."

"I thought you and Chris were planning on staying in NC, though."

She shrugs, too nonchalant. "I don't want to turn a good school down because of Chris. He understands." But she looks away from me, fiddling with her phone.

"How are you two doing, anyway?" I ask.

She chews through another Twizzler before answering me. "We're okay, I guess. He keeps hinting we should have sex soon."

"And?"

She raises an eyebrow at me. "And what?"

"Are you going to? How have you guys waited this long? I mean, you've been dating since I moved here—before, even, right?"

"Yup. Three years. We're just . . . we're just waiting for the right time, I guess," Julia says, but she begins slowly and methodically pulling apart the Twizzler in her hand. "He wants to do it after homecoming."

"You want to, right?" I ask.

"It's not that. I do. I love Chris and I'd be really thrilled if he were my first, I just . . ." She sighs. "I dunno. Like, I'll be making out with him and stuff, and that's great, but any time I think about having sex or we try to go any further, it's like . . . not like a light switches off, really, but I'm just not interested. And it's not just Chris," she adds. "Like when I look at any guy. I've hung out with you and you'll look at a guy and tell me you'd like to get in his pants, and I can look at him and see he's attractive, but . . . nothing." She sniffs. "But I don't know how to tell Chris. Not that I think he won't be understanding, but what if there's something wrong with me?" She wipes her eyes on her sleeve. I dig around in my backpack for a pack of tissues I've kept since the funeral, and she blows her nose.

"Thanks," she says. "I mean how does it feel for you? You and Trent had sex, right?"

"We did," I say.

"So . . . what was it like? You weren't . . . I mean, you enjoyed it, right?"

"Oh. Yeah," I say. "It was great. I dunno if you want details or anything, but it did feel good. And I really wanted to do it."

"And I don't want it at all," Julia says, trying to sound like she's joking. But she just looks miserable. "Maybe I should go see a doctor."

"It's different for everyone," I say. "You could just not be ready?"

"But I'm supposed to be, right?" she says, more to herself than me. "That's what is supposed to happen."

"Is it?" I say. "I thought girls weren't supposed to want sex at all."

Julia laughs, and rolls her eyes. "No, you're right. Sluts if we do, prudes if we don't, yeah?" She shakes her head. "Which would make me the frigid bitch, I guess."

"As if anyone would call you that," I say. "Come on, I'm definitely more of a bitch than you."

At this, Julia laughs out loud.

"But you're okay, though, right?" I ask. "I mean. Chris isn't pressuring you or anything?"

"No," she says firmly, and squeezes my hand. "I'd tell you if he was."

"I'd kick his ass."

"And that's why you're the bitch," she says, and this time, I laugh. But it immediately feels wrong—how am I sitting here, laughing, how am I even *allowed* to laugh right now, to even be happy when Maggie is dead?

If Julia notices my laugh sounds off, she doesn't say anything. She leans her head on my shoulder and pulls apart another Twizzler.

"So," she says through a mouthful. "You interested in

anyone? You're officially out of the rebound period—you and Trent have been broken up for almost a year, right?"

"Yeah," I say. "We have."

Here. Right now. I could tell her about Maggie. I could do it. I could say that I haven't dated anyone at school but that doesn't mean I haven't been dating anyone. I could say that.

But I don't. I don't, because explaining about Maggie would mean coming out, would mean telling Julia about us, admitting that the dead girl is the girl I loved, and how can I do that now that she's gone? How can I tell anyone about us at all when she isn't here to do it with me? I couldn't even come out when Maggie was *alive*.

Mia goes through her radical transformation to look like a real princess and I steal a strawberry Twizzler from Julia and we fall asleep before the movie ends.

I dream about Maggie.

SIX DAYS G O N E.

When I walk in the next day, Dad's eating a sandwich at the table, dropping crumbs onto his laptop. Bysshe is curled up by the chair, trying to act like he's not waiting for Dad to throw him a piece of ham.

"How was your mother?"

She ceased to be Mom after the divorce. Now she is just my mother, like he never had any sort of relationship with her.

"Fine."

"New boyfriend around?"

"Brett? Dunno. Didn't see him."

"How long do you think for this one?"

I shrug. "Hard to tell without meeting him."

It's our own private joke, mine and Dad's, though Dad would never admit to it—we bet on how long each boyfriend will last. It's petty. Selfish.

But she chose booze over us, so. All's fair in divorce and dating.

"By the way," he says, turning back to the table and picking up a stack of brightly colored brochures, "these came for you. And a coach from Jefferson called."

"Oh," I say, drying my hands and taking the brochures from him. "Did you schedule a visit with Jefferson?"

"That's your responsibility, Corinne. And I don't know if you'll be with your mother that weekend."

"You're supposed to know that."

"You can do this yourself," he says.

But I don't know how to explain how unsure I am that I even want to do cross-country in college, so I keep my mouth shut.

"I'll call them back tonight," I say.

"Good," Dad says. He indicates the brochures, which I begin to flip through—Jefferson, Chapel Hill, UNC Greensboro, Villanova—

That last one makes me pause.

"We can't afford any of these schools, Dad," I say. "Maybe Jefferson. And they're all Division I, and I—"

"That's what your scholarship will be for," he says. "And there's no problem with them being Division I. You're good enough."

But I'm not. And even if I was, I can't see myself at any of those schools. I can't see myself at Villanova, not now.

Dad's looking at me expectantly and there's pride on his face and suddenly I know I can never stop running because if I stop running, then that pride goes away.

And so does one of my only ties to Maggie.

The kitchen is too small. The house is too small and these brochures are going to burst into flame if I hold onto them for too long, the Villanova one especially.

"I . . . you're right," I say, and he beams, and I clamp down my apprehension about being unsure about college because the last thing I ever want to do is disappoint my dad.

"I'm going for a run," I say.

"Do you want me to time you?" he asks.

"I—not tonight. It's just going to be casual," I say, and before Dad can protest I dash upstairs and tie on my sneakers, pull my hair back with Maggie's scrunchie, and run.

There's a bite in the air as I step outside, the temperature dropping more now that September's settling in. I stretch quickly, then start off around my neighborhood, heading for the hill at the top.

My legs burn, my calves are on fire, but I push myself up the hill and I keep going. I keep going even though everything inside me is screaming at me to stop, because that's what I need right now. A clear head and sore calf muscles.

I pause at the top to catch my breath. This hill, small as it is, makes me miss Colorado. I miss being a kid, back when everything was simple and my parents were together and sledding felt like flying. Where Dad would push me down the hill in our old neighborhood and I would scream until there was nothing left in my lungs but cold and snow and happiness.

I breathe, think about what Julia said, about going for State. About how Maggie wanted to. About how no one knows what she meant to me except her brother and a girl whose existence makes me feel—I don't know.

I could try for State, this year. I could do it for Maggie, because she wanted me to be better this year, and if I get State then I could get a bigger scholarship, I could get out of here, I could become what my dad wants me to be, what *she* wanted me to be.

I start to run down the hill, push myself as hard as I can. Running down this hill doesn't feel quite like flying, not when I'm trying to pace myself, but it's sure damn close.

I just hope my wings don't burn up in the sun.

I shower off after my run, then put on pajamas and curl back up in bed. I open Maggie's Instagram, careful to avoid the comments on her photos, scrolling down, looking for—what? But then I see it. Way down on her page, a photo of Elissa, sitting outside some coffee shop, laughing and trying to hide her face with her hand. Maggie tagged her in the photo, so I go to her profile.

Unlike mine, unlike Maggie's, Elissa's page isn't private. It's wide open for the whole world to see. There are photos of her at Pride, decked out in rainbow gear, glittery rainbows on each cheek. There are photos of her kissing a brown-skinned girl who might have been her girlfriend. I scroll for pictures of Maggie, for any evidence of the two of them together, but it looks like Elissa only really started posting after she left high school.

I haven't talked to Elissa since the funeral, but right now I need someone to talk to, someone who knew Maggie.

I call her. It takes her a few rings to pick up.

"Hello?"

"Elissa? It's . . . it's Corinne."

"I know," she says. "I saved your number."

"Oh . . . oh, right," I say.

Silence.

"Did . . . did you want something?" she asks.

"I just—did Maggie ever talk to you about running?" I ask. "Because it—it really meant a lot to her and that's how we met, running, and I just . . . I wondered if she mentioned it."

For a second I'm afraid Elissa's going to laugh at me, or worse, hang up. But she doesn't.

"No," she says. "Do you want to tell me about it?"

I do. God. More than anything, I do.

So I tell Elissa. I talk to her about how much running meant to Maggie, about how she took it so seriously, not just because she was good at it, but because she actually felt connected to it. I tell her about how she wanted me to be good at it, not just to follow her, but because she loved it and she wanted me to love it, too. I tell her about how this year was supposed to be the year we were fast shining girls together, making plans to go to schools in big cities where we could be out together, where she was supposed to go to State.

"And now she can't, and I—I don't know, Elissa, but I feel like—I feel like I have to try to, for her? Even if that sounds ridiculous."

She takes a minute. "It's not. To be honest . . ."

"Yeah?"

"It sounds like something Maggie would do."

The hurt that's been lodged in my chest since I found out she died loosens, just a little.

"Our next meet is at Leesboro," I blurt out, not knowing why I'm telling her this. "If you—if you wanted to know."

"I live near there. Do you want to come over after?"

"Yes," I say, and we exchange goodbyes before I hang up, not quite sure why I just agreed to see Elissa again, to even hang out with her, but then I think of what she said, of *it's something Maggie would do*, and I know it's because being able to talk about Maggie with someone who knew her makes it feel like—

Like she still might be here.

EIGHT DAYS G O N E.

Haley's already at work when I get there, mousy brown hair pulled back and shoved under a baseball cap with *Coney Island Ice Cream* written across the front. She's on the phone when I walk in, chatting excitedly with someone and pointedly ignoring me.

It's not that we don't like each other. We just don't know what to do with each other. Haley's more ambitious than I am, more callous about her ambition than Julia or Maggie. I've never seen someone else who *wants* so much and will work as hard to get it.

She hangs up the phone and looks over at me.

"Who was that?"

She shrugs. "No one important."

"Any customers?"

"Absolutely none." Haley pushes herself up onto the counter. "I don't see why we keep this place open in fall anyway."

"I mean, I would complain, but paycheck, so," I say, and she sighs.

"Guess you're right. Though I mean, it's not like I need it anyway, I just like earning money to spend or go out or whatever."

Jealousy flames in my gut, just a little. I do need this job. I'm the one buying all my cross-country equipment, uniforms, sports bras. Saving to buy clothes to look like the girls on the team so I look like I belong, saving for the future I'm not sure I want.

"Guess I don't have that luxury," I say flatly, and Haley almost looks guilty for a minute, but she doesn't say anything else.

We sell two scoops of ice cream in one hour, to a lanky black teenage boy who orders vanilla and a short girl with him with blue hair who's as pale as Haley who orders cookie dough. They tease each other like they're friends, talk about shipping our ice cream to their friend who's in college in New York.

As soon as they leave, my phone rings, some unknown number with a 336 area code.

"Hello?" I say, turning my back to Haley.

"Is this Corinne Parker?" A woman's voice crackles on the other end of the line, mispronouncing my name—kah-REEN instead of what it should be, kor-IN. I let it slide.

"Yes," I say, cradling my phone between my ear and my shoulder.

"This is Alma Holt; I'm the coach at Aldersgate College. You have a minute?"

"Yeah, I do," I say, turning my back to Haley.

"Wonderful. How are you today?"

"I'm well."

I wish my voice would stop shaking.

"That's good to hear. I'm going to cut to the chase, Corinne. How many official visits have you had?"

"None," I say then immediately wish I hadn't because what if that makes me look bad?

"That's all right. I'd like Aldersgate to be your first one."

"Ma'am?" I say.

"I watched your highlights reel. We're interested in you; we think you have potential. Let's schedule an official visit if that's all right with you."

"Of course," I say.

"Does two weekends from now sound good?"

"Yes ma'am," I reply automatically. It's not like I have a schedule to check anymore, not like I have to work around seeing Maggie.

"Perfect, we'll see you then," she says. "I'll put you in touch with Sneha, one of our students, and she'll email you all the information about your visit. Expect an email from me as well, okay?"

"Okay."

"See you then, Corinne," she says, and hangs up before I can even say goodbye. I stare at the phone in my hand for a second.

"What was that?" Haley says, coming around and looking over my shoulder at my phone.

"I think that was my first official recruiting call," I say, and I can't stop the grin from forming on my face.

To my complete surprise, Haley reaches out and high-fives me. "That's excellent! Where?"

"Aldersgate," I say.

"That's cool—they're like Division III, right?"

"Yeah. Which . . . I dunno. Which might be what I need."

Saying my own lack of ambition out loud feels weird. But Haley just nods.

"How many places have you been recruited?" I ask.

"Mm, four? Maybe five. Not half as many as Julia," she says, and there's this note of bitterness in her voice.

"More than me," I say, and she laughs.

"Not like that was hard."

"Hey," I say, and okay, yeah, I'm slightly wounded, but not as much as I probably should be.

"C'mon, Corinne. We both know your heart isn't in it," she says. "You just don't want it as bad as we do."

Once upon a time that comment would have infuriated me, and I would have spent the next practice and race just trying to outrun Haley. Once.

But she's right. My heart isn't in it. It wasn't before, and now?

Now my heart is with a girl in a coffin in the ground.

But that girl wanted me to be better, she wanted my heart to be in it, so I could keep running with her. So for her, I'll try.

Maybe my heart should be in running more, since it's the only thing that's getting me out of here.

My heart should be in a lot of things more; there are a lot of things I should want more than I do.

But wanting is difficult and painful, and I am such a fickle girl.

"You know, if you ever want more hours . . . you can have mine," she says, a tentative peace offering. "And let me know how Aldersgate goes?" She turns back to the counter, leans her arms on the glass of the ice cream machine.

"Yeah," I say. "I might do that."

SEVEN MONTHS BEFORE.

We leave the restaurant in silence, scarves high on our necks to protect against the wind chill, noses red in the cold. Downtown Raleigh is filled with people, sparkling city lights, and champagne laughter.

Maggie is quiet as we walk to her car, bellies full of Italian food. Everyone around us is laughing, holding hands, kissing on cheeks.

I reach for her hand, but she pulls away.

EIGHT DAYS G O N E.

The coach's voice plays in my head over and over as I drive home.

You have potential. We're interested in you. You have potential.

The only person who's ever told me I have potential as a runner is Maggie. She thought I was good enough, thought we could be good enough together.

Do I even want to run in college?

You have potential.

I can't hide the excitement fluttering through my body, bird wings beating in my chest at the thought of being wanted, of being seen as a girl with potential.

Maggie saw me. Maggie *got* me. She didn't laugh when I talked about chemistry or Bysshe or any of that.

If she were here, she'd be proud of the Aldersgate call, not laugh it off like Haley, not pretend I'm settling like Trent did when I texted him. She'd squeeze my hand and she'd tell me how proud she is of me and how no matter where I go she thinks I'm going to do great.

I miss her.

I pull out my phone before I can even think, send a text to Elissa, this girl who knows—

I miss her.

Not two seconds later, my phone dings.

I know. I miss her, too.

Dad's upstairs when I come in, working in his office. I knock on his door, phone still in my hand.

"Yeah?" he says when I come in.

I swallow past the lump that suddenly appears in my throat. How do I tell him I've been recruited? How do I say it? There are so many expectations in this one statement, hopes and dreams and, suddenly, Maggie, her wants and needs and her desire to get far, far away from here—

"I've been recruited."

I spit the words out like they burn, and the heat from them turns my face red and makes my dad's light up.

"Where?" he says.

"Aldersgate," I say, and then he's out of his chair and hugging me and telling me how proud proud proud he is, how excited and he *knew* his school would call me. He hugs me and suddenly I am suffocating under the weight of his expectations.

"Thanks," I say, and it doesn't sound like my voice.

"When's your official visit?"

"In two weeks," I say. "But I don't—"

He pulls back. Looks at me, and there is so much damn pride in his face, and my hesitancy over going falters and dies on my tongue.

How can I disappoint him?

"We should celebrate," he says, like I hadn't started speaking. "Go out. Get a burger. You deserve it, Corey," he says.

Go out. Like old times. Like we're trying to recapture what we were, when I was a girl without secrets and Mom and Dad were still together.

I can't find it in me to say no. To any of it.

"Sure," I say, "Sure. That sounds great. Let me change, okay? I smell like hot dogs."

I take my phone out of my pocket, ready to call Maggie about my dad and Aldersgate.

But when I open my phone, Elissa's last text is there, glaring up at me.

I miss her, too.

And suddenly my hand is pressed over my mouth and I'm choking back tears because I can't cry about this, about her, I can't—not now, even though the ache of missing her is so persistent in my chest.

Dad knocks on my bedroom door. "You ready to go?"

"Yeah," I call, voice shaky, and I hear his footsteps retreating and I swallow down my tears, because I am a girl with potential and Maggie
isn't
here.

NINE DAYS G O N E.

Our third meet of the season is at Leesboro.

I'm shaking before I even get out of the car. This is a course I've run so many times, but never without Maggie in front of me.

I don't know how I can do this today.

But I have to. Aldersgate wants me, Dad's here watching, and I am a girl with potential. Girls who want to fit in and be bright, shining girls? Those girls don't skip meets. Those girls go along with what their dad wants because it's easier to focus on that than any wants of their own. Those girls try to honor their dead girlfriend's memory by going to State, even if they aren't sure that's what they want. Even if the nagging voice inside their head asks, *but is that what* you *want?*

What I want.

I want what I'm supposed to want, and right now, that is to win this meet.

I need to not think about this. Julia is stretching by one of the picnic benches, so I go sit down next to her, ignoring the chatter of the group of moms before the meet starts. My dad's standing off to the side, the literal odd man out. He doesn't know their etiquette, their Southern women code. It wouldn't have fazed Mom. She was the loud one, the outgoing one. They balanced each other like that, and without her, he's kind of lost even though he grew up with half the people here.

That's the other thing about this town. Everyone's family knows everyone, doesn't matter if their kids go to rival high schools. Haley's mother is friends with all the moms from our team and half the women here cheering on Leesboro. We can't go to the grocery store without running into someone we know from school, or work, or Grandma's church.

How can I come out in an environment like that? Even if I only told one person? If that one person told her mom, then everyone would know, and that thought terrifies me, even if I can't put *why* into words.

It's why I haven't told the girls on the team. Because their moms know Maggie's mom, and—

I crane my neck while I stretch. The other moms are all grouped around Mrs. Bailey as if they can shield her from any more harm. Dylan's arm is around her shoulders, like he's helping her stand. I don't see Mr. Bailey, don't know if he's here—why are they here?

Then it hits me that it must be their first real meet since Maggie died, so of course Dylan and his mom would be here, of course they'd be doing something for Maggie. My attention shifts to the Leesboro girls, who are standing huddled by their coach, black armbands around their wrists, armbands they will wear the rest of the season, for Maggie.

I look away. Turn back to Julia, who's sneaking a cookie from one of the Tupperware containers sitting out in front of us.

"Those are for after the race," I say, and she laughs.

How am I doing this? How am I thinking about Maggie one moment and joking with Julia the next? I don't deserve to grieve her if I can forget about her so easily.

"It's fuel," Julia says, waving it in my face before chomping down on it. "I need it."

"Please, like we don't both know you're going to come in first," I say. I nudge her. "Oh, by the way—I got a call from Aldersgate yesterday, about a visit!"

"Wait, seriously?" Julia grins. "Corinne, that's great news!" She stops stretching and stands so I do, too, as she pulls me into a hug.

"I'm sorry I didn't text you. I wanted to tell you in person," I say.

She pulls back. "Hey, don't worry, I get it! Remember when I told you about Clemson?"

"Julia, you drove to my house at two in the morning to tell me."

"Exactly," she says, grinning.

It was over the summer, one of the days I wasn't spending with Maggie, because she'd gone to the beach with her family.

I almost told Julia then, almost blurted it out because I wanted to share that part of my life with her, but I didn't. She was so happy about school, and I didn't want to spoil the moment, though all I thought about when she left was how Maggie had gotten recruited by Clemson too, and how I wasn't getting any calls, and how Maggie had said that senior year I needed to step it up, get better, train with her in the summer so we could go to the same places together.

You're talented, but you just don't push yourself, Corinne.

It was the first time I'd seen that critical side of her, and I resented her for it, just a little.

But I worked harder. I promised her I'd be better.

And now I have to be, even if she isn't here to see it.

Julia hugs me. "We should go out to celebrate after," she says.

"I can't today," I say. "I, um—Mom wants to actually hang out, so I should . . ."

I shouldn't be using Mom as an excuse like this, but Julia won't know.

"Oh. Okay," Julia says. "Maybe some other time?"

I nod, but over her shoulder I see—

Dylan.

He catches my eye and jerks his head toward the bathrooms, away from everyone else.

I can't let Julia see.

"I'm gonna go find a bathroom before the race," I say lamely, and she nods, winking at me before grabbing another cookie on her way to talk to Coach.

Dylan is by the parking lot when I reach it, calling my name, a sharp two syllables in the September air. I glance around to make sure no one sees me talking to him.

"I'm about to race, Dylan, what do you want?"

It's mean, I know, but I can't help it. How can I tell him his eyes look like hers and I can't see them without missing her, without that profound ache in my chest?

"I just . . . I wanted to check on you."

I look at him, and he sighs. "No. That's not it. I—I mean I do want to check on you, but I also wanted to tell you—there's a bonfire memorial for Maggie tomorrow. The seniors, some of her friends. I thought you might—might want to go?"

Do I want to go? Surround myself with everyone else's grief, let my own feed off it, surround myself with people who knew her when they don't know me?

"Elissa will be there," he says.

"Why does that matter?" I ask.

He holds up his hands. "I'm just saying you should talk to her." He sighs. "I know . . . I know you and I aren't close and I know I can't tell you what to do, but you and Elissa both lost someone important to you and it might help if you talked about it. That's all."

You lost someone important to you.

God, I can't think about that. Can't think about how much she meant to me, not now, not when I'm about to run, not when I have to run better than I ever have. Even though I'm doing it for her.

"We are," I say. "Talking, I mean."

"Good," Dylan says. "Okay. Well."

There's the sharp blast of a whistle, and I nearly jump out of my skin.

"Good luck today," Dylan says as we part and head back toward the starting line. He looks like he wants to say more, but doesn't.

I wonder how many times he said that to Maggie before a race.

I really can't think about that, though. My head is so full of everything and I just—need to focus on this race and running and the trail in front of me.

I win our race.

Not Julia.

Not Haley.

Me.

I run, and I run, and I know she isn't ahead of me this time but I keep running, because she isn't here to try for State and I have to do it for her.

I have to.

TWO MONTHS BEFORE.

It's really hot outside and I'm perched on the bleachers, watching Maggie run laps around her high school's gym.

It's summer. We should be spending lazy days at her neighborhood pool, in her basement, doing something where we're tangled up in each other. Instead, she's training. I'm timing her as she runs, as she pushes herself to be better, faster, best.

At least eight coaches have called her already, and senior year hasn't even started.

I watch her run as she becomes a blur around her gym.

She wants this. She wants it more than any other person I've ever met, and she makes me want it, too. She makes me want to be better, faster, best. We've been training together some. But she always beats me, and I'm starting to not be able to take the look of disappointment on her face.

That's the thing about Maggie that I didn't have with Trent. I liked Trent, but we never pushed each other. What we had was easy, simple, good. It was not better, faster, best.

But Maggie . . . Maggie wants us to be better. Faster. Together at a huge college running Division I, holding hands as we walk down streets.

And I want that because she wants it. She makes me want it.

There's a distant echo as the door to the gym opens and Dylan steps in. Before I can stop him or say anything, he comes and sits next to me on the bleachers, skinny pale elbows resting on his knees.

I fidget with the hem of my shorts. This is only the third or so time I've seen Dylan since he caught us together. I still have no idea what he thinks of me.

But there's pride in his face as he watches his sister, and maybe we have that in common.

"She's good, isn't she?" he says, watching as Maggie makes another lap.

"Yeah," I say. "Yeah, she is."

We don't say anything else. We just watch as she runs, as she completes lap after lap, over and over and over, running in circles and trying to be better.

NINE DAYS G O N E.

Sweat drips into my eyes as I get in my car, even though I cooled down after the race. I can barely believe I did that, can barely believe I ran like that. I haven't run like that since . . .

I can't remember. Since summer, maybe, since Maggie wanted us to be better so we could go to the same schools.

I text Elissa. **Hey, are we still on for this afternoon?**

She responds only a minute later. **Sure, yeah. My house? I'll send you the address.**

She texts me the address and I plug it into my phone, listen as an automated voice tells me to start heading down Highland Ave. She only lives five minutes from the park.

Julia waves at me as I pull out of the parking lot, smiling.

What would happen if I told her?

Elissa lives in a shotgun-style house, tan, front-porch, Southern. She's on the porch when I pull up, long brown legs crossed and bare feet resting on the rail as she smokes a cigarette.

My car rumbles on the gravel of her driveway and she flicks the cigarette out.

"You came," she says. Then, "Hey."

"Hey," I say, easing myself out of the car, still in my running clothes. I can feel her eyeing me, and I blush.

Stop it, I chide myself. There's no reason she'd be thinking about me like that.

And I'm here to talk to her about Maggie, anyway.

It feels weird, being here. Maggie hasn't even been dead two weeks and here I am, walking up to the front door of her ex's house, to do . . . what? To talk? To hang out? I don't even know if I want to do any of those things, but I'm here.

"Sorry about the mess," Elissa says as she opens the front door and I follow her inside.

Her house is far from messy. Even though there are a few dishes in the sink, it's certainly cleaner than my mom's place has ever been. It's kind of empty, too, with clearly secondhand furniture and a TV stacked on top of a few crates.

"I haven't had time to decorate; I just moved in," she says to explain.

It clicks. "Wait . . . this is yours?"

She laughs. "Yeah. What, you thought I still lived with my parents?"

The answer is obvious, so I don't say anything.

"It's easier if I'm paying for it. That's why I'm doing community college, too," she says. "I've got a roommate to split the cost, but she's hardly ever around."

"What's she like?"

"You," Elissa says casually. I can feel my ears turning red.

"How's that?"

"Athletic and pretty," she says, and it takes me a minute to register the *pretty* part of that.

"Your parents were okay with this?" I manage as I maneuver around her living room, looking at the pictures she and her roommate have tacked to the wall.

"I mean, they aren't paying for it, so yeah," she says. She sits down on the beat-up couch. "They weren't too happy about me moving in with Cassie, but I guess they were right on that front."

"So she's not just your roommate," I say.

"No, she is," Elissa says. "We broke up."

"That's gotta be awkward."

She shrugs. "It is what it is."

"Still," I say.

"It's only awkward when she brings someone home. This place has really thin walls," she says, and I find myself blushing again.

A photo catches my eye—one from Maggie's Instagram, printed out and put in a frame, Elissa and Maggie with their arms around each other.

Seeing them together, happy, is a punch to my gut.

"Sorry," Elissa says, coming up behind me and laying the photo down. "I forgot that was there."

I nod, swallow past the lump in my throat. "Why didn't she tell me about you?" I ask, turning to face Elissa.

Pain flashes across her face, just for an instant, and I wonder if I really want to know the answer to that question.

"I don't know," she says. "I mean, she was really private, but . . . I don't know."

"You're out, right?" I ask, and I surprise myself at the bitterness in my tone.

"Yeah, I am," she says. "Not to everyone, but enough people. I mean, I live with Cassie, and she used to get mad if I lied and said we were roommates even though it was sometimes safer."

"Oh."

Elissa looks over at me. "Hey, do you wanna get out of here? We can still talk about Maggie, but—I dunno, maybe a change of scenery would be good."

I sniff. "Yeah, okay. Can you drive?"

"Sure." She smiles at me. "I'll just get my keys."

I fidget, standing in her kitchen while she runs to her bedroom to grab her stuff, playing with my phone.

Why am I doing this? Why is *she*? We've barely spoken, barely even know each other.

Elissa reappears with her keys looped onto her belt on a carabiner, smiling at me. "You ready?"

I shrug. Her face falls.

"Hey, Corinne, we don't have to go anywhere if you don't want."

"It's not that." Suddenly I'm desperate for her to understand. "It's not that, I do want to, I'm just—why me, I guess? I haven't been that nice to you."

At this, Elissa shrugs. "You're grieving. Your girlfriend died, Corinne. You can be angry about that."

"Yeah, but that doesn't explain why you—"

Elissa holds up a hand. "I . . . I dunno. I thought about what it would've been like for me if Maggie had died when we were together and I didn't have anyone to talk to and so—I don't know. You just look like you could use someone who understands what you're going through."

Something in the way she says it hits me, and I deflate, because she's right. Being at school, being at practice, having to pretend everything's normal—it's just been so fucking suffocating.

But Elissa understands. She gets it, and right now, that means I can breathe.

"Okay," I say. "Let's go."

Forty minutes later we're at a small cafe in Durham, signs in Spanish and English on the walls and warm churros on a plate in front of us. We didn't talk much on the drive over; instead, Elissa put on a band called Heart.

"They're my mom's favorite band," she said. "Saw them when they played here with Joan Jett—honestly, it was really badass."

"I don't know them," I confessed, and Elissa rolled her eyes before turning up the music louder. It's the kind of music I like, wailing guitars and loud vocals, the kind of music Maggie hated.

Elissa texts me the links to their performance at the Kennedy Center when we sit down. "Sometimes if I come down to visit Dylan I'll come here," Elissa says as she sets her coffee cup down.

"I didn't know y'all were that close," I say.

She shrugs. "We were friends before I dated Maggie. Stayed friends after."

"How did he feel about the two of you dating?" I ask.

"Same way any older brother would about his little sister dating, I guess."

"And he . . . he didn't have a problem with it? That you . . . you're both girls?" My face feels hot even as I say it.

Elissa shakes her head. "If he did, he kept it to himself. He never did want to upset Maggie."

I look down at my coffee. I'm jealous, I realize, jealous that Dylan and Elissa are so close, close enough that he would call her the day Maggie died, and all I get are scraps, even if—

Can't think that.

"Can we talk about something else?" I ask, and she nods.

"Sure. How's school?"

"Not that," I say, and I laugh. Elissa smiles and looks down at her coffee, nearly the same as that picture on Maggie's Instagram.

Maggie.

What am I doing? Talking about school with Maggie's ex when I didn't even know she had an ex, drinking coffee like nothing is wrong. I am here and she isn't and—

"Excuse me," I say, and push back from my seat and rush to the bathroom. Thank god it's a single stall.

I lock the door and press my hands over my face, hard, turn on the sink so no one can hear me crying. Guilt stabs at my insides, because Maggie is gone and I am here and somehow, that doesn't seem fair.

"You okay?" Elissa asks when I emerge from the bathroom a few minutes later. I know my face is red, my eyes are puffy, but I wave her off.

"Yeah. I'm okay."

"Okay," she says, and she doesn't push it. "So. I know you don't want to talk about school. Which is fine, I can tell you about my classes if you want, but—there's also an arcade down the street we could go to? Get your mind off things?"

I shake my head. "Tempting, but . . . I think I want to stay here."

"Afraid I'll kick your ass in air hockey?" she asks, and to my surprise, I laugh.

"Air hockey, yes, but I'll totally crush you at Ms. Pac-Man."

"Did you memorize the pattern?"

I nod. "And when to eat the fruit."

"Badass," she says. She grins. "Didn't realize you were a closet geek."

And there it is again, that *I wouldn't know that by looking at you.*

But then again it just feels like everyone who does look at me only sees what they want to.

"Mom would take me to play Pac-Man," I say. "Back in Colorado. Well. We'd go to the movies and she hates previews so we'd always just play games instead until it was time to go in for the movie. I couldn't grip the controls because I insisted on eating popcorn before playing so everything was always really greasy. But like, that weirdly made me better at it."

"Huh," Elissa says. "That's cool. My parents used to make my sister take me if she went out with her friends, so I got really good at air hockey since all the teenage boys she hung out with taught me. I could kick their asses before too long."

"Please tell me before each game you pretended you didn't know what you were doing to lure them into a false sense of security."

"You know it," she says, and I grin.

"Ruthless."

"You bet."

"What . . . what does your sister do?"

"She was in law school but then decided she wanted to be a rabbi instead, so she's studying for that," Elissa says. "Mom and Dad weren't super thrilled, but they don't have to pay for law school now, so I guess it's okay?" She shrugs. "Dani seems super happy though."

"That's—wow. She and Dylan would get along."

Elissa rolls her eyes. "I can't get them together; they start arguing about theology and it's all downhill from there."

"Yikes." I twist my hands together.

"It's fine," Elissa says, smiling. "My sister's always been that way—she'd make me debate her at the breakfast table before she'd drive me to school, and she's the one who helped me with the reading before my bat mitzvah."

I nod. "Did—did the four of you ever hang out, I mean?"

"Nah, too awkward," Elissa says. "Dylan and I have stuff in common, and Maggie and I, but all four of us hanging out would have felt like a forced double date even though Dylan and Dani are *so* not interested in each other," she says, and she smiles. "Plus in my experience your siblings don't always want to hang out with whoever you're dating."

"I wouldn't know," I say. "Only child."

"That's rough," Elissa says. "Wait—shit—I didn't mean that. I just meant—I dunno. I can't imagine my life without my sister."

It seems to hit her, then, the reality of what she just said—she can't imagine life without her sister and now Dylan has to.

Elissa clears her throat and looks down at her watch. "Do you—do you want to go home?"

"I probably should," I say. I reach for my bag to pay for my coffee, but Elissa shakes her head.

"My treat."

"But you drove."

"You can get it next time," she says, and the smile she leaves me with starts butterflies in my stomach.

I can't like her. No matter how nice she is, no matter how much she gets it.

I can't.

TEN DAYS G O N E.

The first thing I smell when I pull into the driveway of one of the Leesboro girls' houses is the smoke from the bonfire. Dylan sent me her address, off a road twenty minutes from my high school, her house the only one around for miles, with acres of farmland behind it. All the cars are parked just straight in the gravel in front of her house, several just in the ditch. Judging from the number of cars, Leesboro's entire senior class is here.

Maggie would have loved this. She loved her classmates, loved hanging out with them. She had more school spirit than anyone I've ever met, actually enjoyed pep rallies and football games and the musicals. She loved all of it, and she couldn't understand why other people didn't feel the same sense of pride she did about her high school.

I do not belong here.

I think about getting in my car and driving home, curling up in bed with a fantasy novel and telling Dylan that this was a mistake, all of it.

I step closer to the bonfire.

A small group of people mill around near the fringes, clutching glass bottles of beer. I can see Dylan's red hair illuminated by the firelight, his arm around Elissa.

I pull my jacket around my shoulders and walk up to the football players huddled around the cooler. And it's only then I can see the black armbands they're sporting, same as the girls at the cross-country meet the other day.

I keep my head down as I open the cooler and grab a beer. But there's a hand on my elbow, and I turn.

It's one of the football players, though he looks too scrawny to do much damage. He's got blond hair, spiked up.

"You don't look old enough for this," he says, snatching the bottle from my hands and looking me up and down in a way that makes my insides squirm. "But I guess I can let it slide since you're hot."

He holds the bottle out to me. I reach out to take it, but he pulls it back just before I can, laughing.

I know what he wants me to do. He wants me to be flattered he called me hot. He wants me to laugh, flirt, *haha you're so funny keeping this away from me.*

"Give me the fucking beer," I snap.

His face darkens, and he leans so he's in my face. "Make me," he says, and my hands curl into fists because I just want my damn beer and I don't even want to be here, and then I hear a voice.

"Ezra, give her the beer before I break the bottle over your head," Elissa says.

"I was just kidding," he says, rolling his eyes and handing it to her. She takes it from him and thrusts it into my hands.

"He's a dick," I whisper as we head to the bonfire, but the tension doesn't leave her shoulders.

"He's always been like that. A lot of those guys are," she whispers back. Her hand finds mine and she squeezes once before letting go to sit down at the edge of the bonfire, folding her long legs up as I sit down next to her. No one even looks at me except Dylan, who gives me a small, almost imperceptible nod. Everyone else is staring down into their beer.

They are all grieving, and so am I, but glancing around the bonfire I still feel so outside of them. We are all grieving different versions of the same person, and I—

I'm the only one who doesn't deserve to.

I shouldn't have come here.

I clench the bottle in my fist and take a large swallow to clear my head. It tastes awful, like watered-down piss, and fuck, how does anyone drink this?

But I need to drink; I need to forget. For one night I want to forget about running and Maggie and Julia and Aldersgate and Dylan; I want to forget who I am, who I was. I can feel Elissa watching me as I pour the beer down my throat, but she doesn't say anything.

"Does anyone have a story they want to tell about Maggie?"

Dylan asks, his voice too loud.

Everyone tenses. No one wants to talk about it, about her, no one wants to disturb her ghost even if her brother said they should.

"I'll go," a girl says, Southern accent thick, blond hair hanging iron-straight down her shoulders and glowing as orange as Dylan's in the light. "I'm Casey. Maggie and I stage-managed the musical together freshman year."

I half-expect everyone to chorus, "Hi, Casey," like some Alcoholics Anonymous meeting. The thought makes me want to laugh, and I take another sip.

"Freshman year we did *The Sound of Music*," Casey says. "And Maggie was our assistant stage manager. And she was—I dunno. She was so good with the kids, because we had actual kids playing the Von Trapps—Mrs. Henderson's daughter Jessica was Gretl. She was adorable. And Maggie—God. She'd be SO serious if one of the actors talked backstage, and then at the same time she'd help Jessica with her lines and it was like, there was this whole other side to her personality when she was working with kids. She was great, she . . . she really woulda been a fantastic teacher," Casey finishes, and her voice breaks and everyone stares at the fire awkwardly until one of the other drama girls takes Casey's hand.

Another girl stands up, dark curly hair pulled back from a pale heart-shaped face.

"I'm Alison," she says. "I've known Maggie since we were in

kindergarten. We go . . . we went to the same church."

She launches into another story, about how she always envied Maggie because she was so nice, how jealous she was of her when they were both in middle school and Maggie dated Trey Zhang.

I can't hear this. I can't hear any more of these stories, stories about who Maggie was and how wonderful she was, stories about the side of her I never got to know.

Because that's what this is. No one's going to talk about how she talked in her sleep or how grumpy she was in the morning, no one's going to talk about how she'd push herself to the point of tears when she was running, no one's going to talk about the time she yelled at a freshman for not getting up to speed. These stories will turn her into a perfect girl who loved kids and wanted to teach and only dated boys and I will be erased and forgotten and so will the parts of her these people don't know about.

I stand up before I realize I'm doing it and can feel everyone's eyes on me.

"I'm Corinne," I say. "And I—"

Dylan is staring at me like he might kill me. Elissa's face is stone. Everyone else is looking at me like they've suddenly realized I'm there.

I can't do this. If I tell them it will ruin whatever image they have of her, and I—

I can't say it about myself. I want to but I can't, because if I shatter the image they have of her, I don't think Elissa or Dylan will forgive me, and I'm not sure I'll be able to forgive myself.

And I don't deserve to grieve her with these people anyway.

I sit down. And the silence is awkward and tense until one of the boys clears his throat and begins to talk about how great Maggie was again.

I pick at my nails, drink my beer, and keep my mouth shut and traitorous heart hidden.

By eleven, most everyone's left, the bonfire reduced to a small flame. The football players have begun a drunken game, and some of the girls have left to watch them. It's only me, Dylan, and Elissa. We stare into the bonfire like it'll give us answers, because we don't have anything to say to each other.

Elissa's hand is inches from mine.

I try not to think about it. I feel warm and I don't know if it's from the fire or the beer or her, I don't know.

Should I know? I feel like I should. I feel like I should have known Maggie loved kids and wanted to teach.

But maybe everyone else around this bonfire should have known about us.

And suddenly there is too much weight on me and too many thoughts turning around in my head and my stomach and I mumble something and run to the edge of the woods to throw up.

Maggie's gone, Maggie's dead—

Someone's hand is on my back, rubbing, soothing, and I cough.

"Hey, it's okay."

Elissa. It's Elissa.

She's touching me and I hate that's my immediate thought when I'm throwing up at the edge of the woods behind some girl's house at a memorial for my dead girlfriend.

"You all right?"

I cough, and I let her put her arm around my shoulders and guide me toward a tree, away from the dying bonfire and the football game and the ghosts. And I'm sitting in pine straw and Elissa is sitting next to me and I can feel the warmth of her body next to mine and for a moment I forget I had a girlfriend at all, for a moment I let myself forget that Maggie is dead, and I look at the girl sitting next to me with the short hair and the boyish face and—

I want to kiss her.

The thought comes out of nowhere but suddenly it's there all the same.

I want to kiss Elissa.

But I can't want that. Not here. Not now, not ever. She is my girlfriend's ex, my *dead* girlfriend's ex, and being attracted to her would just be—

It would be wrong.

"I miss her," someone says, and it takes me a minute to realize it's me. And then there's a warmth on the other side of me and Dylan's sitting down next to me and my face burns like he can hear my thoughts about Elissa, about his sister, and Elissa's hand covers mine and Dylan sits next to me and I cry for what I've lost.

Dylan drives me home, says I can pick up my car later.

I spend the entire ride with my head on Elissa's shoulder, Dylan glancing at us in the rearview mirror.

But she doesn't pull away.

And I don't either.

ELEVEN DAYS G O N E.

I wake up at home. In my bed, forgetting for a second where the hell I am and what's happening and—

The bonfire. The Leesboro reunion, crying on Dylan and Elissa.

I look down and I'm still in my clothes from the night before and I wipe my hand in front of my face and it comes away black and streaked. Shit.

It's six o'clock. Friday. I still have school, still have practice, still have to make it through today, I still have to—

I jump out of bed and shuck off my clothes, jeans and top and underwear that's—red. Fuck. On top of everything my period has come. I grab a pair of plain black underwear from my dresser and automatically take two ibuprofen from the bottle on the nightstand and pop them. Seven days of moodiness and bleeding and even though I'm a runner and it helps, the cramps are still going to let me know they're here by tomorrow.

I stuff six tampons in my bag, not because I need that many but because it's inevitable some other girl on the team will be on her period, and I know what it's like to be the girl without a tampon or pad and how embarrassing it is, so I always pack extra.

I pull a sports bra over my head, wince at the tightness against my chest, and go ahead and put on leggings and a sweatshirt because who cares what I look like today.

My phone buzzes while I'm shimmying into the leggings. Dylan.

You coming to the game tonight?

I frown down at my phone. **Game?**

Dylan responds about five minutes later, the world's slowest texter.

Our homecoming game is tonight. There's a memorial for Maggie. More formal. You can come, sit with me and Elissa.

I swallow hard, suddenly. Not because he's inviting me but because do I actually want to go, do I want to do this?

I think about Elissa, think about the way she looked last night, brown skin illuminated by the firelight and hair freshly undercut and those eyes watching me the whole time and I think about wanting to kiss her and I—

am not supposed to think that. I'm going to Maggie's memorial service tonight, my girlfriend who hasn't even been dead two weeks. Why the fuck am I thinking about kissing another girl? Why am I thinking about kissing girls at all?

Maggie was the first girl I ever kissed. Maybe the first girl I even knew I wanted to kiss.

I am not one of those girls who knew when they were five years old that something was different about them. Maybe I should have. But no girl ever caught my attention before Maggie.

After—after I noticed her at that first meet, though, I took notice of girls, girls I never would have glanced at before. And like with Maggie, my stomach flipped and my palms got sweaty and it was like, shit, when did all these girls become so cute?

I had never even wanted to kiss a girl before Maggie, but after the thought wormed its way into my head it was all I could think about. Kissing Maggie. Kissing other girls, boys, whoever. Just . . . kissing.

NINE MONTHS BEFORE.

She invites me over the day after Christmas so we can hang out. I tell her I'll come, after I visit my mom. (Separated parents should mean twice the presents, but it doesn't. Just a nice Christmas with my dad and one with my mom that feels like an afterthought.)

It's a balmy sixty when I pull into Maggie's driveway, which shouldn't be allowed. Winters in Colorado meant heaps of snow and cold, icy wind in your lungs. Winters in North Carolina, I've come to learn, can either mean an inch of snow that shuts the whole state down, or almost spring-like weather.

Today feels like spring. I'm in a dress I dug out from the back of my closet I wore last year to Julia's birthday, three-quarter sleeves in a soft pink color.

I don't know why I've dressed up to come over to her house.

This is only the second time I've seen her since I told her I broke up with Trent. She called me later that night to talk about it, asked if I was feeling okay.

I said yes. I was the one who broke it off, after all, the way I have with every other boy.

She said good. She was happy for me.

We didn't talk much after that, but when I hung up there were knots in my stomach.

I've been thinking about it more and more—about her more and more. About what it would be like to be with her. What it means—if it has to mean anything.

What if it's just Maggie? What if I'm only attracted to her? What does that mean?

Does it have to mean anything?

Fuck.

I wish I had someone to talk to about this.

But if I tell Julia, if I talk to her, that will make it Mean Something. And I'm not ready for that yet.

I grip the steering wheel tighter.

Maggie's house is huge, certainly bigger than mine. She has a front porch and columns, old-school Southern charm. There are no cars in the driveway except hers, but I try not to think about that.

She opens the door and immediately hugs me, curly hair pulled back in a ponytail. She's in a T-shirt and a pair of shorts that must have been her brother's.

"Hi," she says, pulling back and tucking a stray strand behind her ear, her face suddenly red. "Did . . . did you have a good Christmas?"

"Yeah," I say. I don't look directly at her, and she looks down at her feet. I'm still standing on her porch.

"Can I come in?" I ask, and she laughs nervously.

"Yeah. Come on, let me show you around."

She doesn't, though. We pass by grand rooms and she just tosses out what they are—kitchen, living room, dad's office. We stop at the door to her basement—or "bonus room," as she calls it. The second we step in I immediately understand why she calls it that. It's not a basement like at my house—concrete floor and boxes from when we moved. It's got carpet, a couch, a pool table, and a large TV with a crap ton of video games.

I follow her down the stairs.

Does it embarrass her, having all this stuff? It would embarrass me, but she seems almost comfortable in it.

That's the thing about her—she's comfortable in any environment. Running, coffee with me. She's at ease, all smiles and charm, and I'm the girl standing awkwardly to the side who doesn't know what to do with her hands. Sure, I'm not that way at school, where I know my place (with the girls on the team, by Julia's side), but put me somewhere unfamiliar?

Forget it.

Maggie sits down on the couch, tucks her feet up under her, and begins fiddling with the remote.

"So, um, get anything nice for Christmas?" I ask as I sit down on the opposite end of the couch. She shrugs.

"New running stuff, mostly. You?"

I shrug. "Um. Dad got me some stuff from Colorado you can only find there—snacks and stuff."

"Do you miss it?" she asks earnestly, looking at me with wide eyes, like she really wants to know.

She leans forward. And I look up at her for the first time and my gaze immediately lands on her lips.

What am I doing? A girl is sitting in front of me and I like her and I don't have a boyfriend and I'm sitting here talking about Christmas like it's the most important thing in the world and—

There is a whole freaking couch cushion between us, and I want to kiss her.

"Sometimes," I say, and look down at my hands, at her purple couch, because if I don't—

The couch squeaks as it shifts, and I look up and she's moved so she's sitting right next to me, and I—

I'm staring at her lips again.

"Corinne," she says, and her voice is soft and hesitant and unsure, and I lean forward and kiss her before I won't let myself take the chance anymore.

It's quick, a barely-there kiss, but my heart beats frantically like it's trying to come out of my chest.

Her eyes meet mine. I can't read them, can't read her expression because the only thing I'm thinking right now is I kissed her I kissed her I kissed her—

And then—

she
leans
forward
and
kisses
me
back.

NINE MONTHS BEFORE.

She kissed me.
  She kissed me.
  She kissed me.
  And I kissed her back.
  And all I can think on the drive home,
  is how much I want to kiss her again.

ELEVEN DAYS G O N E.

My cramps have started full-swing by the time I've made it to school, and I want nothing more than to put my head down on my desk and sleep.

But the universe isn't going to afford me that chance. I'm almost late to homeroom, and run in just as the bell rings, already irritated.

Julia nudges me with the end of her pencil. "Hey. You okay?"

"Cramping," I mutter, and put my head on the desk. She makes a noise of sympathy.

"Would you want to come over tonight?"

I think about the football game, about Dylan. Elissa.

"I can't tonight, Jules," I say. "To be honest, I'm probably just going to go home and nap."

"I get it," she says, and quickly squeezes my shoulder. "Text me if you need anything?"

It's an echo of what she said to me over a week ago, when I found out Maggie had died.

I don't know why she keeps offering.

SEVEN MONTHS BEFORE.

I'm home from Maggie's around eleven, Mom already asleep. She doesn't wait up to ask who I was out with, and I'm grateful for that.

Well. Grateful and sad.

I kick off my shoes and head to bed, lying down on top of the comforter and scrolling through my messages. Julia's name is at the top, and I flinch at seeing it, because we had plans tonight: we were supposed to hang out with the girls from the team and watch a movie.

Hey, sorry I had to cancel.

A bubble immediately pops up indicating that Julia's typing, and I hold my breath.

No problem. wish you told me why.

I swallow.

The screen in my hand, glowing blue.

I had a date—

I'm dating a girl—

I can't do it. I can't tell her.

My facade, my life here, it is all so perfectly constructed. I am not a girl who likes girls. I am a girl on the cross-country team, a girl with an ex-boyfriend she is still friends with, a girl with straight A's, a girl you want to be.

And it's not that I don't trust Julia; it's not. She's my best friend and I trust her, but part of me thinks—would she get it? And then part of me thinks, I can't lose her. Not over this. If I tell her, there is the possibility of losing her, and I can't face that.

Plus, I don't know how Maggie would feel about it—me telling someone else about us. We haven't talked about it, not really, and we've only been together two months and thinking about telling anyone just feels so *big*.

Hypothesis. If/then. If I keep lying to Julia, then she won't be my best friend anymore.

If I come out, then everyone will treat me differently.

How many times can you tell your best friend no before she gives up on asking? Before she stops being your best friend anymore?

If you are hiding a huge secret from her, if you don't tell her everything, is she even your best friend?

ELEVEN DAYS G O N E.

Julia doesn't talk to me at lunch. If Chris notices, he doesn't say anything, and Trent is nowhere to be seen. I don't see him until five minutes before third period starts, when he waves at me from the other side of the hallway.

A few junior girls look at me when Trent comes up to me, jealousy plain on their faces.

"Hey," he says, smiling that golden-boy smile. He holds out a plastic bag from the local drugstore. "Got you this."

I take it from him. Inside is a bag of dark chocolate, my favorite, and a tub of Epsom salts.

"I heard you telling Julia your . . . you know, your *thing* started," he says.

"Oh," I say, surprised that he cares enough to do something. "Thanks."

"No problem," he says. "See you around, Corey."

He gives me a quick wave and then he's off.

I wish I could tell him to stop calling me Corey now that we aren't together.

But I look in the bag at the stuff he got me, and I know I can't.

Julia doesn't talk to me in chemistry, either, not even when I try to slide her a chocolate. Mr. Wilson lectures about carbon and balancing equations and I decide it'll be futile to try to talk to Julia, so I go back to taking notes and paying attention.

I like chemistry. I like the math and the structure and finding out the smallest order of things. If I can dissect it, neutralize it, break it down into the smallest atoms, then it will make more sense.

"What's unique about carbon?" Mr. Wilson asks, and my hand shoots up.

"It bonds to itself and other elements," I say.

He nods. "Good, Miss Parker. I guess you could say carbon is bisexual, right? It goes both ways."

My face reddens before I can stop it.

"The sluttiest element," someone jokes in the back, and there's laughter. Even Mr. Wilson cracks a smile.

My fingers tighten around my pen. In front of me, Julia snorts, and Haley is giggling into her hand.

I am not a slut, I want to say.

But I'm too much of a coward, and these people don't deserve to know, right? Even if some of them are my friends.

Julia laughing along with this hurts, and I know if she knew about me she wouldn't, but if this is her reaction . . .

I swallow the lump in my throat and I hate it, but I laugh along with everyone else.

SIX MONTHS BEFORE.

"I think I'm bi."

I say it again.

"I think I'm bisexual."

Take a breath. Look in the mirror. Say it again.

"I'm bisexual."

I burst into tears.

FIVE MONTHS BEFORE.

I think I can say it.

I think I'll be able to say it to Maggie.

We're at that park she loves, sitting together on the swings. Our knees are touching. We're not swinging.

The metal chain is cold in my fist. Maggie's been talking nonstop about doing something for our anniversary this month, coming up with big dreams and plans.

I push away from her, sneakers scraping the dirt as I push back and start swinging.

"You're quiet," she says. "You're never quiet. What's on your mind?"

I shrug.

I should say it. I should tell her I've found a word that fits, a word that describes what I feel for her and for the boys I've dated.

But instead I swing higher, higher until I'm far away from Maggie and the realities of telling her.

She's waiting when I come back down. Maybe that's the best thing about her, but sometimes it's the thing that makes me feel like I could never, ever deserve her.

I take a deep breath. Wrap my fingers through the chain link of the swing.

"I . . . I think I'm bisexual. I'm bisexual," I say, and I swallow down the lump in my throat and the fear in my voice and hope she can't tell.

She reaches over.

She holds my hand.

"I'm glad you found a word that fits," she says, and she kisses me. Never mind we're out in the open, never mind anyone could see us.

She. Kisses. Me.

And I kiss her back.

ELEVEN DAYS G O N E.

I text Elissa immediately after practice, heart thrumming in my chest as I turn my back to the other girls and shield my phone.

Are you going to the football game?

I change quickly, hoping my phone doesn't buzz while Haley's still around.

But the locker room slowly empties and Elissa still hasn't texted me back and I almost give up and am walking to the bus since my car's still at the girl's house when—

Can't stay but I can drive you.

Okay, then.

Okay.

Elissa pulls up to the girl's house we were at last night, her fingers twitching by her sides, and I know the second I leave the car she's going to pull out a cigarette and smoke it on her way home. Maybe smoke two. We've barely spoken the entire ride there.

"So should I just follow you to the game?"

She shakes her head. "I'm not going. And it's Shabbat, so I should really go to synagogue." She shrugs. "I don't know."

I nod. I don't get faith, religion, but now . . . now seems like the time I might.

"Thanks for driving me."

"Hope your car's still here," she says.

I scan the area for my Volvo. "It is."

"Good."

I unbuckle my seatbelt but don't move to get out of the car. "Elissa . . ."

My voice is raw, and she turns, and she looks at me. We haven't spoken about the bonfire, about the way we've been looking at each other because if we speak about it then it means there's something to acknowledge.

"What?" she says.

I want to kiss her. She's looking at me and I want to kiss her, because she is the only one in the entire fucking universe who understands what I'm going through, and because she listens to me, and because she looks at me like Maggie did, like what I have to say *matters*, and this time I don't stop myself, this time I lean across the passenger's seat and press my lips to hers.

She tastes like smoke, like grief. She kisses me back and my hands move to the back of her neck and I kiss her and I kiss her and—

She wrenches away from me like she's been stung. "Get out," she says, her voice hoarse.

"Elissa . . ."

"Get out of my truck right now," she says. "Corinne. Please. I need you to go."

"But—"

"Get out!" she snaps, and her voice breaks and I scramble for the door and nearly trip getting out of her truck but I'm able to make it out, my shaking hand still pressed to my mouth, like I can still feel her kissing me, and I don't know whose lips I'm thinking about, hers—

or Maggie's.

I pull into Leesboro's parking lot ten minutes later, parking away from the other cars, and head toward the football field. It's easy to find Dylan in the bleachers, his hair difficult to miss in the crowd. There's a wide berth around him, like no one wants to sit next to him just in case their own sister dies. I can feel everyone from Leesboro looking at me as I make my way up and sit down beside him.

"You came," he says.

"Yeah," I say.

"Elissa not with you?"

The mention of her name is like thorns curling around my chest. "She said it was Shabbat."

"Shit, I forgot." He shakes his head. "She never went out in high school, either. I can't believe I forgot."

"It's okay," I say. "I mean. She drove me to get my car but she just went home."

He nods. "Fair enough."

He's distracted, I can tell. My eyes follow his, where he's watching the cheerleaders stretch and warm up, the marching-band kids milling around on the field. I want to ask if he misses her, but it's obvious that he does. Everyone around us is laughing and talking and Dylan and I just sit in silence, united by our own grief.

How is everyone just sitting here like she isn't dead? Two weeks ago, these people were pouring their messages out onto Maggie's Instagram, and now . . . what? Now they're at a football game and it's like it never even happened, it's like she isn't even dead.

I sit with Dylan as the Leesboro students around us cheer for a losing team, as the lights of the stadium blind everyone around us until it's just me and him and the ghost of his sister.

Halftime comes too soon. Leesboro is losing spectacularly, there's no other way to describe it. By halftime everyone is grateful for the break, though I can feel the anticipation of the students behind us as someone makes their way to the podium to announce the homecoming king and queen.

The woman who steps up is short and squat, with a wild

blond bird's nest of hair I can see from here is filled with too much hairspray.

I've never understood that about Southern women—the overuse of hairspray and blue eyeshadow. And it's definitely a Southern thing, women in the Midwest didn't really dress like the ones I've seen down here.

She pulls a paper out of her pocket and there's a collective holding of breath from the other students, like their lives depend on who's going to be crowned homecoming king for this year.

The woman clears her throat. "Your king," she announces grandly, like she's on some sort of game show or introducing real royalty, "is Ezra Miller. Your queen is Savannah Welch."

The skinny football player who wouldn't give me a beer steps up to the makeshift stage, a pretty girl with bleached blond hair on his arm. Typical. This is so, so typical.

They're given their crowns and the band plays some half-hearted song and the students around me mutter. Apparently Ezra and Savannah aren't that popular.

The woman clears her throat again, and everyone around us falls silent. My hand finds Dylan's and squeezes.

"Leesboro lost one of our own this year," she begins, and my throat closes up. "Maggie Bailey was a bright student who had a full scholarship to run cross-country for Villanova next fall. She was a member of the drama club, the cross-country team, stage-managed the school musicals, and sang in the choir at her church on Sundays. She was a friend to so, so many of you, and a wonderful student, and sister, and daughter, and we're going to miss her dearly," the woman concludes, tears shining on her face, her frizzy hair illuminated by the stadium lights.

"We will proceed now with a moment of silence before our chorus sings *Amazing Grace*." The woman steps back from the microphone and the chorus shuffles forward.

They barely get through the first verse before someone starts crying, one of the sopranos trying to sing through her tears. By the time they get to the third verse the whole stadium is singing along. Most of us are crying.

Dylan and I just stand there, holding hands, dry-eyed while the rest of the world around us mourns a girl none of them knew like we did. When the last notes have died in the air, the chorus trails off the stage like lost little ducks, and the woman with the frizzy hair steps up to the microphone again. She takes a minute to compose herself, wiping at her eyes dramatically even though she wasn't crying, then, greets the rest of the crowd with a beaming smile and declares the game back on.

Dylan and I part ways without saying much to each other, not like there's anything to say at this point. He walks back to his car and I walk back to mine and it's only then I let myself think about kissing Elissa.

Why did I do that? Maggie's barely been dead two weeks; I shouldn't be kissing another girl, let alone her ex. Never mind that she's out and brave in ways I'm not, never mind that I think she's cute or handsome or whatever; my girlfriend is *gone* and I shouldn't—I shouldn't be having these feelings for another girl.

God, I miss Maggie. I miss her being here, I miss kissing her, I miss how she made me feel.

I'm afraid without her. So much of myself for the past year was wrapped up in who I was with her. I liked who I was then. I liked who she made me become, that I was not a snarky bitch, that I was not a disappointment, that I was just a girl she loved, a girl she thought was good enough.

And without her I don't know how to be that girl again.

I drive home. I go in. I lie to Dad.

I shower.

I lie in bed and think about kissing whoever and think about sex and slide my hand down between my thighs and

I

stop

thinking.

FOURTEEN DAYS G O N E.

Practice Monday is brutal. By the time it's over I'm drenched in sweat and my legs are aching.

But I feel—good. Like I haven't in a while. Maybe it's the endorphins from running or the feeling that I actually did well, maybe.

At any rate it gets my mind off Elissa and the fact she hasn't called. Or texted. Or the fact that I kissed her.

I need to stop thinking about how I kissed her.

I linger in the locker room, take my time getting dressed because I don't want to think about going home and starting my chemistry homework or calculus or anything else.

As I'm pulling my sports bra over my head, Julia enters, cheeks flushed peach under her tawny skin. I turn my back to her and clasp my bra, though it's not like we haven't seen each other change a thousand times.

Fuck, I need my best friend.

"Julia?"

"Mm?" Julia says as she peels her socks off and lays across the bench in just her sports bra and shorts.

I clear my throat. "I . . . I'm sorry."

She sits up, fixes her dark eyes on me. "Go on."

"I . . . I'm sorry for being so distant. The past couple months, I mean."

Her face softens. "You know I wouldn't be so damn mad at you if you'd just tell me why you've been avoiding me. I know there's a reason."

I look away from her. There is a reason, but it's too big to tell her right now.

"Want to come to the homecoming game with me Friday?" I say, and her eyes narrow at the change of subject and I'm afraid she's going to go right back to being mad at me. "Please? We can watch Chris and Trent play." The unspoken *like we used to* hangs in the air. "We can get ready at my dad's house and you can spend the night after if you want."

"I told Chris I'd stay with him," she says, and there's something unspoken there, too. It's homecoming, and she's a football player's girlfriend.

"We can still get ready before the game, can't we?" I say, desperate, extending the words like a peace offering.

She turns and looks at me and finally cracks a smile. "Yeah. I'd like that."

The tightness in my chest loosens up a little more. I've missed having Julia by my side. I've missed having anyone by my side.

"Oh, by the way," I say. "My Aldersgate meeting is this weekend."

"You'll love it," she says. "I've loved my visits so far."

"You still haven't told me about those."

"What do you want to know?" she asks.

"Um. Everything? Anything that'll help me prepare?"

She nods, looks down at her watch. "I've got some time now before I'm going home, do you . . . do you want to hang out?"

It's both a challenge and a question in one.

"Yes," I say, and the grin that splits her face lights me up from the inside, because God, I've *missed* my best friend.

"Downtown?" she asks, and I laugh, because it's a joke that started between the two of us, way back when I moved here— I'd asked Julia to show me around Leesboro, hoping to find hidden gems, something under the small-town facade, so when she'd promised to show me downtown I'd been excited.

Turned out, downtown was one stoplight, a church, a shop that kept changing every two months, and Tito's Pizza, where an old arcade was hidden in the back. First time Julia took me there I kicked her ass at Ms. Pac-Man, and even though I'd complained about "downtown" being so small, any time Julia'd offered to take me there, we ended up at the pizza joint, grease on our fingers and quarters heavy in our pockets for games.

"Let's go," I say, and she links her arm with mine.

And just like that, I'm forgiven.

If only it were that easy with everyone else.

After Julia and I get pizza I walk across the street to the ice cream shop, hoping to talk to Amber about my schedule, if she can up my hours. I need to pay for gas and my sports bras are wearing thin, and any hours she can give me would be great.

Haley's sitting outside on the bench when I pull up, phone to her ear.

"No, Mom, I'm not," she says as I get out of the car. She rolls her eyes and looks at me before mouthing *My mom* and walking off.

I head into the shop and grab my apron from below the counter and tie it around my waist, jam my ponytail through a pastel-colored hat. I can see Haley through the window, hands gesturing wildly as she paces back and forth. She finally comes back in a few minutes later, mouth in a line, thin eyebrows knit.

"Everything okay?" I ask. Her frown deepens.

"Just my mom," she says. "Asking about Regionals when I don't know yet and apparently Hilary knew by this time so why don't I?"

I know Hilary. Everyone from our school knows Hilary, Haley's older sister by two years, the track star now on a scholarship at Notre Dame. Hilary is our shining example of What Can Happen If You Work Hard Enough. Our teachers bring her up all the time, because we all know what the alternative is.

Here is the alternative, the example we are not supposed to strive for: girls I know who sell Avon with Mom, fresh out of high school and settled down with their sweethearts, already pregnant and selling makeup to make ends meet. Dad told me before that the only way he got out of here was by being smart enough to get that scholarship to Aldersgate and then meeting Mom, or else he'd be stuck in the town farming and living two miles away from his parents, just like his brother does.

Here's what they won't tell us, though. Those girls? The ones who sell Avon, who live with their boyfriends, their parents only a few miles up the road? They seem genuinely *happy*.

I wonder what it's like, for Haley. The rest of us just have to hear about Hilary. She has to live in that shadow.

Maybe that's why she tries so hard.

Haley sighs. "I just wish my mom would be happy with me, you know?" she says sourly.

I don't know what to say to that. I want my mom to be unhappy with me, then at least it'd mean she was paying attention.

"I mean, Coach hasn't even said anything about Conference, let alone Regionals," I say, trying to make her feel better.

"Which I tried to tell my Mom, but she insisted that if I were better I'd have heard by now. Like Coach would've given me some special treatment or something—and you know how ridiculous that is."

"Yeah, I do."

She's silent for a few more minutes, staring down fuming at her phone.

"For what it's worth, I think you're good enough," I say quietly.

She looks over at me. "Mean it?"

"Yeah," I say, and nudge her with my shoulder. "Why do you think I'm always trying to beat you?"

"Hah," she says, but she nudges me back. "You're all right, Parker."

"Gee, thanks," I say.

She smiles. "Would you maybe wanna sit together at the homecoming game Friday? I mean I know you'll have Julia with you but if y'all want to sit with me and some of my friends, you can," she says.

"Yeah," I say. "I'd like that."

She grins. "Good. You excited about the game? Watching Trent play?"

I shrug. "I guess. I mean. We broke up like a year ago so there's not a ton to be excited about."

"Why did y'all break up?" Haley says.

"He got too serious," I say, turning back to her.

"Too serious? Trent?"

"I know," I say. I push myself up on the counter, turn Maggie's scrunchie over and over on my wrist. "I liked him. I really did. And what we had was good, but then he started talking about plans for the future and me coming over to meet his parents and I . . . I got scared. It felt like too much. So we broke up."

Haley nods. "Yeah. I get that. It's funny, isn't it? Most people would say guys are the ones scared of commitment."

"Ha. Yeah."

I keep turning the scrunchie. Maggie wanted those things, too. She wanted college and meeting parents, but for us it was different. Being with her would've been some big, declarative statement, not just about my sexuality, but about us.

Isn't that what I wanted, though?

Didn't I want to be with her?

"Corinne?"

"Sorry, lost in thought," I mutter. I stop fiddling with the scrunchie and hop off the counter, and I'm about to say something else to Haley when something catches my eye outside.

It's Elissa. Outside. Laughing with some girl—her roommate?

And then she turns, and I can tell she sees me. And before I can react or move or do anything, she grabs the girl's arm and steers her away.

Haley watches the whole exchange without saying anything, and doesn't ask me about it after.

Maybe I misjudged her after all.

EIGHT MONTHS BEFORE.

All I can think about is her. Thank God the season's over, or else I know this would be affecting my running.

She texts me in January, asks me to meet her at the park by her high school once she gets out of theater auditions.

Are you auditioning?

Can't sing. Stage-managing, so I get to watch.

Good luck.

Everything is new with her. Every text makes me grin like an idiot. I've become one of those girls who doodle initials of their crush in the margins of their chemistry books.

Julia texts me as I'm pulling up to the park, asking if we can maybe hang out this weekend, because we haven't properly hung out since the season ended.

But Maggie asked if I would go to the movies with her this weekend, and how could I say no?

Later, Jules, I say, then put my phone in my pocket.

I'm abandoning my best friend for a girl. I never did this to her with Trent.

But she knew I was dating Trent, and I can't predict how she would feel about me and Maggie when I barely know myself.

I've never been to this park before, but I find it easily. It's not difficult to find things in Leesboro, once you know where they are. Though I guess our town in Colorado was the same way. Small towns with secrets are the backbone of this country.

I am a girl with a secret.

(I am a secret.)

Maggie's car isn't there when I get to the park, so I pull into the gravel by the swing set and get out. It's finally cold enough I feel at home, cutting wind at my back.

I sit on one of the swings and wait for her, my phone in the pocket of my sweatshirt. The metal chain of the swing chills my fingers, but it's a comforting sort of cold. I always did like this weather better.

Gravel crunches as Maggie's car pulls up, and my heart starts beating faster, though I don't know if it's from nerves or seeing her. There's no one around at this park—it's too cold—and anyone driving by would just see two girls on a swing set, talking.

She has her hands in her pockets as she starts walking toward me, head bowed.

I want to kiss her, but I'm afraid to.

She takes a seat next to me on the swing, twirls around in it.

"Hi," she says.

"Hi," I say. "How were auditions?"

"Good. We know who we're going to cast," she says. She looks up at me, bites her lip. This is the first time we've seen each other since Christmas. Since we kissed.

What if she says it was a mistake? That it was all a mistake, and she doesn't really like me, and she's not even into girls and and and?

I reach over and take her hand.

"What did you want to talk about?"

She's quiet, the only sound the creaking of the swings as they hold our weight. "Us," she says after a moment, and my heart beats faster because there is an us.

"I like you," she says, and twines her fingers through mine. "A lot, Corinne."

"I . . . I like you, too," I say. "And I don't—I don't know what I am and I'm trying to figure that out but Maggie, I *really* like you, and—"

She kisses me again. Leans over across the swing and presses her lips to mine, her mouth soft and cold.

"Do you . . . do you want to maybe try this? Us? Dating?" she asks, and I kiss her back, hoping she knows what my answer is.

EIGHTEEN DAYS G O N E.

Friday comes too fast, our whole school buzzing over the football game. The cheerleaders wear their uniforms all day, blue and gold ribbons tied in their hair. Even the teachers lighten up; Mr. Wilson spends chemistry class talking about the compounds that come together to form a football, and the English teacher, Ms. Shafar, has us watch *Remember the Titans*, because nothing says school spirit like watching a small Southern town try to overcome racism through football.

Julia comes over to my house to get ready for the game so we can go cheer on the boys. She's curled her dark hair and pulled it back into a high ponytail. She looks like a cheerleader. I tell her so.

I've hidden every pamphlet from Aldersgate, Oklahoma, and everywhere else in the back of my closet. Tonight, I don't want to talk college, or recruitment, or running. I want to gossip about boys with my best friend. I lounge on my bed while Julia does her makeup, resisting the urge to look at my phone and text Elissa.

She hasn't talked to me since last week. Any texts I've sent trying to apologize have been ignored.

I shouldn't have kissed her. It was a bad idea, and now I'm close to losing the one person who understands what I'm going through with Maggie.

"So, you doing anything fun after the game?" Julia asks.

"Mm, like what?" I ask.

"Oh, I don't know," she says slyly. "Maybe trying to get back together with Trent? It *is* homecoming."

Last homecoming Trent and I had sex in the bed of his truck while it was parked in his backyard, and all I could think about then was how good it felt and how romantic it was, and all I can think about now is that it was freezing and I fell asleep using him as a pillow because he forgot to pack one.

"I'm not getting back together with him. That's over. It's done."

Julia huffs. "He might expect it, you know, since you're clearly not talking to anyone else."

Here would be a good opening. Here. Right now. I could tell her about Elissa, about Maggie, I could tell her I'm bi.

But I don't.

"I really don't care what he expects," I say. "And who cares if I'm not talking to anyone else? Who says I have to be dating someone all the time?"

But I do.

"Anyway. Chris wants to go out and celebrate after

homecoming, which for him means getting a large order of chili cheese fries from Cook Out, then I have to spend the rest of the night begging him to brush his teeth before we start making out," Julia says. She swipes on a coat of lip gloss, checks to see if any is on her teeth. We don't talk about how she might have slept over with me, if she wanted. It's homecoming. We both know where she's going when the game is over, regardless of whether we win or lose.

"How're you feeling?" I ask.

"About the game? Excited. Hopefully we'll actually win this year."

I throw a pillow at her. "I wasn't asking about the game."

"I know." She sighs, averts her gaze from mine in the mirror. "I mean I know we're probably going to have sex tonight, so it's not like I'm going to worry about it or anything. And I . . . I do love him, and he makes me feel good," she says, blushing. "So . . . I dunno. I think I'm ready."

"You don't have to pretend to be ready if you aren't," I say.

"No, I . . . I want to. Don't look at me like that," she adds. "I really do. Chris is a great guy. I love him. I want to have sex with him."

Her eyes never meet mine.

"Your Aldersgate visit's tomorrow, right?" Julia says as we pull into the parking lot.

"Yeah."

"You excited?"

"I'm excited."

"You're going to text me every second, right?" she says.

"Of course I am," I say. "I'm staying Sunday night too so I don't have to drive back—I've already told Coach—but I'll tell you everything when I can?"

"Duh," she says.

We step out of the car, gravel under our feet. Our nails are blue and gold, and Julia grips my hand as we walk up to the football field.

We sit with the other cross-country girls, all chattering excitedly before the game starts, gossip floating through the air on feathers with razor-sharp edges. I hear whispers about how Soledad Evans is sleeping with the quarterback of Green Hill Catholic Prep's football team, how Hilary Russell is failing her sophomore year at Notre Dame.

If this is what they're saying about these girls, what would they say about me?

But I can't think about that tonight. Tonight, at least, I actually belong with these girls and at this game and at this school. Tonight it isn't an act. Tonight we are not Corinne or Haley or Julia, tonight we are long-hair, shiny matching ponytails. We are gossip and chipping fingernail polish and sleepless nights spent worrying over boys.

We cheer, loud, as the boys break through the butcher's paper. We've painted our faces blue and yellow and our class rings glint in the stadium light. There's nothing individual, not here, not tonight. We're all out on that field with the boys, and we're all responsible if they win or lose.

This is it for these boys, and they know it. We all know it. Only a few of them will play football in college; and we're all never more acutely aware of that fact than tonight. If they're good enough, if any coach sees them as an underdog story they'll be lucky. But some of them will work at the gas station up the road and at least one of them will die drunk driving home from prom, and you wish these things wouldn't happen, but they do.

God, I don't belong here, I never belonged here in the first place, my accent isn't the syrupy sweet drawl of these girls', it's the clipped hard syllables of a Colorado winter. I do not have a boyfriend on the football team, not anymore. I have a girl I might like and a girl no one knew anything about.

Chris gets tackled by someone from the opposing team—who are we even playing?—and Julia grips my hand and shrieks.

Julia needs to get out of here. Chris needs to get out of here. They are the lucky ones. If they stay they'll say it's by choice but we'll all know the truth—that as good as they are, even they couldn't get out.

Truth.

No one knows the truth about me and Maggie except Elissa, and suddenly that knowledge is a weight on my chest and I can't be in this stadium with these screaming girls anymore.

"I'm going to the bathroom," I tell Julia, and she nods and lets go of my hand and keeps cheering for her boyfriend with the rest of the cross-country girls who won't even notice I'm gone.

SIX MONTHS BEFORE.

"We should start thinking about colleges," she says.

Her hands are still in my hair, her lips still inches from mine. I don't want to talk about college or the future or how the hell we're going to get out of this small town; I just want to keep kissing her.

"Later," I say.

"No, not later." Maggie stands up, pulls away from me, and I fall back onto her lavender comforter as she moves to her desk and opens her laptop. "Where are you getting recruited to?"

"I don't know yet."

"No one's called you?"

She can't keep the shock out of her voice.

"I'm not as good as you."

I can't keep the hurt out of mine.

"I'm sure they will." She leans back, squeezes my hand. "You're great. And then we'll get out of here and we'll be able to be together. It'll be great, won't it? Big city, being out . . ."

What is this? I want to say. *We're here right now, we're together right now, what is this?*

But we're not out, not here, and I know, really, that's what she's saying.

So I don't ask.

EIGHTEEN DAYS G O N E.

My phone is out of my pocket before I can even think about it, hands dialing Elissa's number.

God, how fast I've shifted to calling her instead of Maggie.

I'm hiding near the outdoor restrooms, hoping everyone's too engrossed in the football game to come over here, or that the game is too loud no one will hear me call Elissa. Her phone rings, and I pray she'll pick up even though I'm not the praying type, even though she hasn't talked to me all week, I just—I need to clear things up with her.

Her phone rings.

And rings.

And rings.

And just when I think she won't pick up, there's a click.

"Corinne. What do you want?"

No *hello*, no *hi how are you*, no formalities.

What do I want?

I know what I'm supposed to want. I am supposed to only

want boys, to want to come out, to want college and gold medals, and I am not supposed to want Elissa.

I've never been good at knowing what I want, though.

"I . . . I just wanted to talk."

"So talk."

"I—I'm sorry about last week—"

"Not about that," Elissa says, voice rough. "We're not talking about that."

"Elissa . . ."

"Corinne. We're not doing this. I can't, I—not now. It was a mistake, all right? Just a one-time mistake. It's not going to happen again."

My heart sinks.

"I miss her," I say softly. "Elissa, I . . . no one here knows about us and I can't take it and I miss her so much and I've got a college visit tomorrow and she was supposed to do this with me, she was supposed to—"

"I know. I know. I'm sorry," she says. "I . . . I hate to do this to you, but I have to go. Okay?"

I sniff. And before I can say "okay," before I can say or do anything, she hangs up the phone and leaves me alone.

NINETEEN DAYS G O N E.

The drive from my dad's to Aldersgate College takes almost two hours. Two hours I replay my conversation with Elissa over and over in my head, alternate between swearing and singing along to the angriest girl rock songs on my phone—Garbage and Paramore and churning guitars and loud voices.

Maggie hated this music and teased me mercilessly for it. I'd just turn it up louder and sing along, and she'd cover her ears and stick her tongue out and laugh.

Sometimes when I was driving and was focused on the road she'd unplug my phone without warning me and plug in her own, blasting show tunes and singing loudly. She was a terrible singer, but it never stopped her. Last spring, she played nothing but *Hairspray* until I knew every single damn word of that entire show.

She'd wanted me to come see it, see where her hard work had gone because she wouldn't stop talking about how talented the cast was and how proud of them she was even if they drove her insane. So I did. Bought a ticket and sat in the back row, and even if the songs were cheesy, even if it wasn't my thing—I was so proud of her for it.

My phone starts playing something from *Hairspray* and I almost lose it because I forgot.

I forgot she put the songs on there once so I'd have to listen even when my own phone was plugged in, because she knew I didn't change songs while I drove. I forgot she'd done that.

I bite my bottom lip so hard I taste blood and next thing I know I'm crying over one of those cheerful songs and I'm trying to sing along but it's not the same and it's never going to be.

Aldersgate is smaller than I thought it would be, and it's colder, too. The campus is pretty, though, with old brick buildings except for the library, which is a massive stone monstrosity rising out from the center of campus. I park in a parking deck and heave my duffel bag over my shoulder.

I'm supposed to meet one of the girls from the team in front of the library, Sneha or something, or that was the name on the email I received on the ride over here.

There's a girl standing in front of the library who waves when she sees me, so that must be her. She's petite, with dark brown skin and curly black hair pulled back into a ponytail, red glasses framing brown eyes.

"You're Corinne!" she says, and there's no question in her voice. "I'm Sneha—did you get my email? Sorry it was so late."

"Um, yeah, hi," I say. "No problem."

"Do you hug?" Sneha asks.

"Uh—yeah."

She reaches around and hugs me, then pulls back, smiling. "Is all you say 'uh, yeah?'"

"Nah, I'm just—overwhelmed."

"First time on a college campus?" Sneha asks, and I nod. "Well, let's go put your stuff down and I'll give you a small tour. Are you cool with just hanging out in my room tonight? It's been kind of a long week with midterms, and I don't really have the energy to go out. There's a party tomorrow night we'll take you to, though," she says, smiling. "And you'll meet the coach and the rest of the team tomorrow."

"Sure," I say. "That sounds fun."

I get settled in Sneha's dorm room while she goes and takes a shower, glancing around at all of the stuff on her walls. She has a bunch of Georgia O'Keeffe paintings, and a row of rainbow-colored cardigans hanging in her closet, a map of North Carolina over her bed.

Sneha's friend Olivia comes over around seven, pulling a bottle of wine out of her tote bag and winking at me. We order wings and sit around watching *The Great British Bake Off* on Sneha's laptop, laughing and chatting.

And then Olivia's phone rings. She pulls it out, a smile blooming across her face.

"It's my girlfriend," she says, and hops off the bed. "Hey

babe!" She mouths *I won't be long* at us then heads out into the hallway.

Girlfriend. She said girlfriend. And not in the way straight women down here sometimes do, laughing about getting drinks with their girlfriend. She said it like it meant something.

"Girlfriend?" I ask Sneha tentatively, hoping nothing in my voice gives me away.

"Yeah," she says. "They've been dating like, six months now I think? She goes to App State."

"Oh," I say, and look down at my hands. Sneha glances at me curiously.

"That's not like—that's not going to be a problem for you, is it? Because I'm bi, too, and if it makes you uncomfortable to stay with me—"

"No!" I blurt. "No, it's not—it's just—"

I'm bi, too.

It's on the tip of my tongue, but saying it to this girl I barely know, this girl I've only just met, when I couldn't even tell my best friend about it, feels like a betrayal.

But Sneha is patient. She's quiet, and she waits, and maybe I can tell her, this girl I might never see again.

"Are you out here?" I ask, and she blinks, like that's not what she was expecting me to say.

"I am," she says. "Though I have a boyfriend, so not everyone knows. But—yeah, I am."

"How?" I ask. "Like I mean, how can you be out, how is it

here, because this is still kind of a small campus—"

"It is," Sneha says. "But I've found people here, they don't really care. That doesn't mean it still isn't scary to come out to people, but it's been—I dunno, I've had a good experience with it here." She shrugs. "Why?"

"Because I . . . I'm bi," I say, and then bite my tongue because oh my God I can't believe I actually said it, out loud. When I look back up, Sneha is smiling warmly at me.

"Are you out?" she asks, and I shake my head.

"I'm . . . I guess I'm waiting until college," I say. "Or I don't know. I live in a really small town, and everyone knows everyone, and I don't know how they'll react—"

"I'm from North Carolina," she cuts in. "I grew up here. And I know it can seem backwoods, or backward, and parts of it can be, but just—don't discount the whole state, you know? Or the whole South. Queer people live here, too, even in rural areas. And people will surprise you, if you trust them enough to let them." She reaches down from her bed and squeezes my hand. "It might not be as bad as you're fearing, Corinne. But I get it, wanting to wait."

She leans back and unpauses Netflix, and we keep watching *Bake Off* in comfortable silence until Olivia comes back in.

"How's Ruby?" Sneha asks.

"Great!" Olivia says. "She's coming up next weekend."

"That's awesome," Sneha says, and she scoots over so Olivia can join us on her bed. We watch another few episodes before

Olivia says she has to walk home.

"It was nice to meet you!" she says as she heads to the door. "I hope you end up here!"

"Thank you," I say. Olivia hugs me and then turns to Sneha.

"Text me when you get home safe, okay?" Sneha says, and Olivia nods.

"You know it! See you later!" she says, and blows both of us a kiss as she leaves.

We get ready for bed in silence, me brushing my teeth as Sneha unrolls a sleeping bag for me on the floor.

"Hey," she says as I'm tucking myself in. "You coming out to me was really brave. Thanks for telling me."

I close my eyes, swallow down the lump in my throat. "Thanks for listening," I say. "Good . . . good night."

Sneha turns out the light and I curl up on my side, her words echoing my ears.

That was really brave.

But then another voice, Maggie's voice—

I just don't get what you're so afraid of.

I can't think about that right now. Not that, not her, not the guilt swirling around in my chest because I was brave, I told someone, and she wasn't here to see it.

TWENTY DAYS G O N E.

We're up bright and early to train, and when Sneha's alarm goes off at seven thirty it's all I can do not to hide in my sleeping bag until she leaves.

But I have to do this. Dad's counting on me, Maggie's counting on me, everyone is counting on me to run as fast I can toward a scholarship, toward college.

So I drag myself out of Sneha's dorm and head down to the track with her. The other girls are already down there with a tall, older white woman with short gray hair and a whistle around her neck.

"I'm Coach Alma," she says to me.

"Corinne."

"Are you liking the college so far? Sneha treating you well?" she asks, and Sneha blushes behind her.

"Yes ma'am," I answer, and she smiles.

"Good."

I like her already.

Sneha's friendly to me, and some of the other girls are approachable, but there's a huddle of about six girls looking me over and suddenly I feel like I'm in kindergarten again, wrong hair wrong clothes wrong everything.

Maggie is supposed to be here, doing this with me. Laughing and getting along with these girls and making everyone feel at ease with her Southern charm.

But she's not. I am.

And I am not her.

One of the girls standing off to the side eyes me up and down, not in a checking-you-out way but an are-you-a-threat way.

"That's Molly Chu, ignore her," Sneha says, suddenly appearing at my elbow. "She thinks she's too good for this place, and she's just bitter she didn't get recruited to Division I. Don't let her intimidate you."

"Thanks," I whisper back, and Coach Alma blows her whistle as we all line up.

"Just run laps today, ladies. Corinne is gonna show me what she's got, so don't go easy on her."

"Like I would," Molly mutters.

Coach blows her whistle and then we're off, shoes pounding against the ground.

I can't get Maggie out of my head. Every step I take just feels wrong because she's not here taking it with me. She wanted me to do this, my Dad wants me to do this, be better faster best, but if she's not here to run beside me, to push me to do my best, then—what's the point?

I slow down before I realize I'm doing it, and Molly passes me and I run and try not to look at the coach's face as I cross the finish line, because I am Not Living Up to Expectations.

Maybe I don't belong here.

The party is a different story. I can hold my own at a party. When I was with Trent I went to parties almost every week, and I know my place in them. I've drawn green eyeliner on sharp as a knife, blond hair loose and falling around my shoulders. When Sneha and I walk up to the house the music is so loud I can feel it in my bones, and the cross-country girls all hold hands and chatter and giggle.

This. This I could get used to, this feeling of college and friends who are girls, any friends at all. Here I could be out and not give one single shit about what anyone thinks of me.

The thought is freeing and terrifying all at the same time.

Sneha grabs my hand, lacing dark brown fingers through mine.

"Are you excited?" she asks.

"Not my first party," I say, smiling. "I mean my first party at like an actual college campus but . . . never mind."

Sneha nods. "Don't get too crazy," she says. "I'll watch out for you if you want, okay?"

"Sneha's like our wine mom," one of the other girls says, squeezing her shoulder.

"And no one serves wine at these parties. It's all beer." She makes a face. "So I'll be sitting in the corner watching, okay? Come find me if you need anything."

I nod. I don't like the taste of beer either, though I don't say that. I'm not drinking for the taste, not tonight. I'm drinking so the world becomes a blur and so I can forget everything that has happened to me in the past few days.

Ugh. Maybe I am my mother.

I let go of Sneha's hand and shimmy my way into the party. The music is blaring, so loud it hurts my ears and the vibrations fill my body, pounding out a rhythm that's easy to move to.

I smile at someone, take a drink from someone else, and dance.

I am kissing a girl.

Or are they a boy?

I don't know. I don't care. I'm pretty tipsy at this point, and the only things I do care about are my hands in their short hair and their lips on my neck and then their tongue in my mouth and the pleasant buzz from the alcohol that's helping me forget their name, my name, Elissa's name, Maggie's name, everyone's name. All I want to focus on is kissing and how nice it feels to kiss someone I have absolutely no ties to, kiss someone where feelings aren't involved.

There's guilt at the still-sharp edges of my mind, the part not blurred by alcohol, guilt that's asking how I can kiss this person so openly when I couldn't with Maggie, when she just died—

I pull away from whoever I'm kissing and give them a sharp-tooth smile, go to find another drink, drive the guilt back where it belongs.

Instead, I find Molly, drink in her hand and standing with some of the other girls from cross-country.

"Did you see her making out with Alice Mailer? Oh my God. She's just making the rest of us look bad—like be gay, okay, whatever, but don't look like a slut when you're doing it."

My face is bright red. Molly sips her drink. I wait for her to look over and notice me, the plastic cup in my hand now squeezed in an angry fist.

It takes her a minute, but she notices. "Shit, Corinne—I didn't mean you, you aren't a slut—"

Nod. Smile, bared teeth, no lips. "Of course. And by the way, I'm bisexual. Not gay."

Molly wrinkles her nose as I brush by her because maybe my voice is too loud or maybe I'm just too damn angry or maybe I'm not going to get a drink, maybe I'm going to go find that cute girl and make out with her, maybe that's what I'm going to do instead of drinking and I think she knows that.

But I don't do any of those things. Instead, I escape upstairs and lock myself in the bathroom and try not to think about Maggie or Alice or Elissa or Trent or any of the girls or boys I've kissed because I'm drunk and sad and this just reminds me, it just fucking hurts that this is the reaction I'm going to get.

Boys kissing boys, girls kissing boys, girls kissing girls, everyone kissing whoever is such a goddamn big deal, and I thought it wouldn't be in college but it is. Because girls kissing isn't okay unless it's at some drunken frat party where you make out with your friend for the guys and act like it was a joke the next day, because you're not that girl.

I am.

I am the girl who makes out with another girl at a party and discovers she likes it, and I will be eaten alive for that.

TWENTY-ONE DAYS G O N E.

Sneha and Olivia drive me to Waffle House for breakfast the morning after the party, insisting we should all go out together. If Sneha saw what happened at the party, she doesn't bring it up, and I'm grateful to her for that. I trade numbers with them and head on my way, belly full of waffles.

Even if I don't go to college there, it's nice to know these girls, nice to have their numbers in my phone. Even if I never use them again.

Dad grills me on Aldersgate the second I walk in the door.

"How was it? How was the team, how was training, how was my old stomping grounds?" he asks before I've even set my bag down.

"Good," I say, crossing to the sink and pouring a glass of water. My head is still pounding from the party last night, Molly's comment still ringing in my ears.

But it was—

I don't know if I belonged on the team. If I can really see myself there.

But Dad looks so damn proud and so damn happy so I lie to him and tell him I loved it, that I'll definitely give it some thought.

Once upon a time I would have told him how I actually felt, how apprehensive I am about going to college at all because I don't even know if that's what I want, that everyone expects me to want to get out of here—but where would I *go*?

Once upon a time we were a father and daughter who could be honest with each other.

But that was before the fighting, before I became the glue holding my parents together. Before the divorce, where I now have to be the daughter who does not cause waves, where I have to be someone Dad can be proud of and happy for, show everyone how good he's raising me.

He's never told me this, never said it to me, but I know.

"Can I spend the night with Julia tomorrow? I promised I'd tell her," I ask, one foot on the bottom stair so I can head up to my room.

"Y'all will have plenty of time at school to catch up," he says, accent slipping back in. "Besides. Spend the night with her before a meet. We'll save gas money."

I nod. "Yeah. Yeah, you're right."

"And don't forget to call your mother and fill her in. You know she's expecting you to." He says this casually. In the beginning, acknowledging they didn't live together anymore was as difficult for him as me trying to claim my bisexuality. Now he can get through talking about her without choking on it.

"Yeah, I know," I say.

Maybe she'll be excited for me. Maybe we'll go out and celebrate, maybe we'll decorate my room, maybe she'll stay sober.

I wish she wasn't like this. I wish we could do stuff like we used to, like everything used to be. While I'm at it I wish Maggie wasn't dead, wish Elissa would call me, wish I were better friends with Julia, wish I didn't have to worry about college.

None of it's going to come true.

TWENTY-FIVE DAYS G O N E.

I still haven't heard from Elissa. It's been a week since I called her and two since I kissed her and over three since Maggie died, and—

Mom was excited about Aldersgate, more excited than I thought she'd be since she's never been to a single one of my meets.

Brett's car is in the driveway when I pull up—at least I think it's his car; it certainly isn't my mother's. And I realize he probably has to drive her places anyway, since her license is suspended for another two months.

She hugs me as soon as I step in the door, the dogs yapping from her bedroom.

"I put them up; they were giving me a headache. C'mere, my little college-bound girl," she says, hugging me one-armed because her other is holding a bottle by the neck.

"I don't even know if they're going to offer yet," I say, trying to squirm out of her embrace.

I don't even know if I want to go.

"You will, baby," she says, and she heads into the kitchen.

"So . . . where's Brett? That's his car, right?" I ask, trying not to sound bitchy, trying not to sound like I don't know if it's his car or not.

"Yeah. He's out back in the yard. Y'all have met, right?"

"No, we haven't," I say.

"Well, let's fix that! Brett!" she yells (she would say *hollers* because it makes her sound more Southern), and a minute later a white man with short brown hair opens the back door and steps through.

He has tattoos, I realize. Comic panels weaving their way down his forearms in a sleeve. I wonder if Mom's going through a rebellious punk phase. He doesn't look like a pharmacist who calls football on the weekends.

"You must be Corinne; Sandy's told me so much about you," he says.

Sandy? Mom hates when people call her that. Said it reminds her too much of *Grease.*

Why hasn't she told him that?

"Yeah, hi," I say, shaking his hand. He doesn't have a dead, limp-fish grip like the last guy. Already an improvement.

"You go to Ridgeway, right?" he says. "I'm calling football there in a few weeks—maybe you'll be there?"

"Oh, that'd be great," Mom says. She reaches out and

squeezes my shoulder. "We'll make it a regular family outing."

Family outing. My alcoholic mother and her boyfriend. Yay.

"So Sandy tells me you're a runner," Brett says. "Track and field?"

"Cross-country. Short distances aren't really my thing."

"Yeah, how'd you get into that?" he asks as we all sit down around the kitchen table.

"My friend Julia—she was the first friend I made when I moved here. She made me," I say. "I mean—I was going to sign up for cheerleading and she stopped me and told me there was no way, all the girls had known each other since middle school, and running was better anyway." I smile. "I guess she was right."

I don't say why I kept running. Why I'm still running.

"Nice," Brett says, and the three of us stare across the table at each other.

I think this is the most normal boyfriend Mom's had, even with the tattoos.

And that scares me. I know she deserves normal and happiness but all I can think is she left me and Dad for a bottle and a new boyfriend, and she doesn't deserve a nice pharmacist with tattoos.

"I'm going to go do homework," I say, pushing back from the table abruptly before I throw a glass of water into my mom's face.

...

I spend the weekend with Mom, sulk as she and Brett laugh and watch movies on the couch together and ignore the jealousy flaming in my gut that he can make her laugh.

Saturday Trent texts me, inviting me to watch some movies at his place. I know what this means. It's his code for "there's a party at my house but my brother is looking over my shoulder."

I flip my phone around my fingers, debate going to the party. Maybe I should. Maybe I will. It'd be nice—to act like the girl I used to be. It'd be nice to get a little fucked up tonight.

Wouldn't it?

I text Trent back, tell him yes, I'd love to go.

And secretly I'm pissed. At Elissa for not texting me back, at myself for daring to kiss her, at Dylan for not telling me about Maggie and Maggie for leaving without me.

"I'm going to a party tonight," I tell my mom when I go downstairs. She looks at me and grins, because she knows if I'm out partying then I'm looking to drink, and I'm not going to judge her for doing the same thing.

"Want me to help with your makeup?" she asks. She hasn't helped with my makeup since I was twelve, back when she and dad still lived together and I loved having her help me feel like a grown-up. She's always had a knack for it, for finding the right shades and colors, blending them in.

For the first time I think, maybe that's why she sells

Avon—because she likes it. Because it's something she's actually good at.

"Sure," I say. "That'd be—that'd be great."

Her face lights up, and for a moment, she is just my mom, like she was before. She's the mom who went and got pedicures with me and we talked and I could tell her anything.

I wonder if I could. Tonight. While she's doing my makeup, I could tell her about how I'm not sure I belong at college, how it feels like this goal everyone else wants me to have but I'm not sure I want to have it. I don't know where I fit in now even if I act like it, how am I supposed to survive four more years of that?

I could tell her about Elissa, about Julia and Chris, about Trent. About Maggie.

She takes a swig of her wine and sets the glass down. "Wanna go ahead and pick it out?"

I look at the clock above the mantle. "It's only 12:30. Party won't even start till like, what, nine? I'm going to go out for a bit, then I can come back and you can help me."

"Okay," she says. "I'll be waiting! Have fun!"

"I plan to," I say, and walk out the door, leaving my mother on the couch.

I don't tell my mother where I'm going, and truth is I don't even know until I get there. When I arrive, it seems like the most obvious choice in the world. I park my car at the bottom of the hill, in the parking lot by the old park, steel myself against the lump in my throat, and my hands take my key out of the ignition and my feet walk me toward the cemetery.

Maggie is up there, overlooking a run-down swing set and weathered park bench, the same bench we had one of our first kisses at, the same swing set we sat in when we decided to start dating.

I don't know why I drove here, why I bothered to come. Maggie's gone.

But I kissed another girl this weekend, a girl who wasn't her, and that—that feels like a small betrayal. So I need to be here, need to remind myself of what we had, of who she was to me.

I look up at the top of the hill, where a ridiculously large cross is erected, almost gaudy in its size. It's the focal point around here for miles.

I can't see Maggie's grave from here.

I start to take a step forward, toward the bottom of the hill and the steps leading up, and a shiver runs down my spine. I don't like cemeteries; they creep me out. I'd never tell Maggie that when we came to this park, but the truth is if it was after dark I got the creeps.

I don't know if I believe in ghosts, or ghouls, or dead girlfriends who appear at your running meets, but I don't want to stick around long enough to find out.

Plus, it's almost Halloween. Fall does something to cemeteries, that magical time where the dead can rise and anything is possible, like Maggie rising up out of her grave to come to me.

I shake my head, chide myself for being so naïve. Maggie is gone. She's buried in that cemetery near the top of the hill. She isn't coming back. Not on Halloween, not ever.

The wind blows, pushing at my back, a frigid wall pushing me toward Maggie's grave. I balk, stop.

If I see it, it's final, and I'll know she isn't coming back as a ghost. I know this. If I go to her grave I will never, ever see her running ahead of me again.

And I'm not ready to lose her like that. Not yet, anyway.

So I walk to the swing set and I sit on it and it creaks under my weight and I remember, remember, remember until she's sitting there in the swing next to me, going higher than I will ever dare to go.

I stay at the park for as long as I can stand it. I skip stones in the tiny creek that runs parallel to it. I swing on the swing until my lungs burst with frigid air. When I am tired, I run in the small trail that winds behind the park, picking my way through leaves and sticks and ducking under branches. I run for what feels like hours, until my head is clear and there are no ghosts blurring at the edges of my vision.

By the time I get home, the sun is setting. The dogs are yapping at the screen door when I enter, louder than normal, like my mom forgot to feed them . . .

My mom forgot to feed them.

My mom is passed out on the couch.

There is an empty bottle of wine next to her. There is another one on the floor.

My mom drank too much and is passed out on the couch, and I hate that I am disappointed.

"Fuck," I curse as I grab the dog bowls and fill them nearly to the brim with food. I shouldn't have left her alone when she was drinking, shouldn't even be thinking about Maggie and my problems. I *should* have been here, helping her.

I don't know where Brett is. I should have talked to him about this. I should have told him to take care of her. Or, I should have warned him to stay far, far away from my mother and her mess, like my dad did.

Dad.

I pull my phone out of my pocket and call home, hoping he's not too busy to answer.

"Corinne?"

"Dad? Yeah. Mom's passed out on the couch," I say. He swears, and I hear papers shuffle around. "I was going to go to a party."

"It's six o' clock," he says.

"I know."

"She drank that much in an afternoon?"

"I guess, yeah."

"Where were you?" he asks, and I'm suddenly angry.

Where was he when this started? She drank before the divorce and he didn't notice, he pretended like she wasn't his problem, and it wasn't bad at that point so we could all brush off the fact that Mommy had two full glasses of wine with dinner.

I think he liked when she drank.

I think I did, too. It made her fun, at least for a bit.

But her passing out on the couch isn't fun.

"I was out," I snap. "Anyway. She's on her side. She's snoring. I don't think she'll throw up."

"Corinne, you can't just leave her—"

"Then tell me what to do!"

"Just . . . just sit with her until she wakes up. Make her drink some water and go to bed. Where's . . . what's his name?"

"Brett, and fuck if I know," I say.

"Corey—"

"*Dad*," I say.

"I don't want you going out to any party," he says, and I hear the unspoken meaning in his voice. *I don't want you drinking. I don't want you to end up like her.* "Can you stay with her?"

"Yeah. Yeah, I'll stay with her."

"Thanks, Corey," he says. "Just make sure she's okay and you can come home early tomorrow morning. Tonight, even," he adds, like he's trying to make himself less guilty.

"Okay," I say. "See you later, then, I guess."

I hang up before he can say I love you. Before he can say goodbye, even.

I look over at my mother. Her mouth is open and she's snoring. Her hair hangs in her face, a brunette strand falling by her mouth. One of her fake nails has fallen off.

I hate her. I hate that she doesn't see what she's doing to us. That if she wasn't drinking I'd be able to visit more.

This is all her fault, and suddenly I want to blame her for everything. The divorce. All my lies. Even though I know she had nothing to do with it, everything in the world suddenly feels like it's her fault.

I kick at the couch, hard.

She doesn't stir. So I curse, clean up her wine glass, taking a swig out of the bottle. I make a face—it's white wine. I hate white wine.

I pour the bottle down the sink, the dogs barking as I do so.

Then I put a blanket over my mother, set a glass of water next to her, and go to the fridge. I grab the six bottles of wine inside and unscrew the top from every bottle, pouring them down the drain. I want to take the bottles outside and smash them on the sidewalk, but the noise would wake her up. So instead I put them in a garbage bag and carry them out to the recycling bin.

Mom can be proud. I've done my part for the Earth now. And I will leave before she wakes up and I have to face her wrath.

At least then she'll blame it on Brett.

...

Dad doesn't say anything to me when I get home. He's in his office, tinkering with the computer, though I slammed the door loud enough I know he can hear me.

"Mom's fine, thanks for asking," I yell. He doesn't say anything back, but whatever.

Mom is fine. I need her to be fine. I have too much to worry about right now without her not being fine.

Dad comes in, and we look at each other. "You sure?" he asks.

"Yeah. I put a blanket on her and gave her some water. She was sleeping on her side. She'll be okay. I threw out the wine, too, though I don't know how much good it did since there's more around the house, I'm sure."

"It can't be that bad," he says, and I blink at him.

"She was passed out on the couch at six o'clock in the afternoon. I threw out six bottles of wine, and who knows how many more she has hidden around the house! Dad. It's bad."

He takes off his glasses, polishes them on his shirt like he always does when we're discussing her. "Well. You only have to visit her twice a month. Just be grateful it's only a little bit and leave it at that. She's your mother, Corey. She wants to see you, and she's trying."

"Bullshit she's trying," I snap, and his face goes red.

"Corinne—"

"No, Dad—why are we ignoring this? Why are we pretending like she's fine? She's not fine!"

"She's not my responsibility anymore!" he yells.

I step back from him.

Responsibility. Like she's something to be passed around, like she's a burden, like she's not my mother.

"She's not a fucking piece of homework, Dad."

His face reddens even further, a vein on his temple threatening to pop out.

"Give me your phone," he says.

"Dad . . ."

"Corinne Abigail," he says, and I flush because he's used my middle name.

"Sorry," I say, fishing it out of my pocket. "Can you . . . can you please turn it off?"

"Is there something you don't want me to see on it?"

I think of the pictures of me and Maggie I have saved. Her voice mails. The hearts next to her name in my contacts. My texts to Elissa.

There are a thousand things in my phone I don't want him to see.

"Please just turn it off."

He sighs, and for a second I think that he won't, that he'll just leave it on and my heart will be on display for everyone, including my father, to see.

But he switches it off and puts it in his pocket, and I breathe a small sigh of relief.

"I'll give it back Monday," he says. "Two days no phone. You can use your free time to look up colleges," he adds, and I sigh.

"Fine," I say, and stalk off to my room.

Bysshe is on my pillow when I come up, purring. I bend down and dig under my bed, face still burning from my confrontation with Dad.

I pull out my own box of stuff from when we lived in Colorado, sit on the floor. Look at my pictures, my pink diary, flip through entries.

My family was whole once. We were happy once. Things were simpler in Colorado. I was not a girl who ran from her problems, who was too scared to admit she liked girls and boys because she didn't know. My mother was not a woman who drank. My dad understood me, and my grandparents were alive, and the weather was cold and the air was thin.

I want to go back.

TWENTY-EIGHT DAYS G O N E.

Dad finally gives me my phone back the day before Conference Championships, and I use it to make plans with Julia about sleeping over at her place before the meet. She responds with an enthusiastic *yes!!!!!* and a million smiley faces.

I still haven't gotten to tell her about how everything went at Aldersgate. It felt like too much just to tell her at lunch.

There's another message waiting for me when I finally turn my phone back on, one from Elissa that just says,

hey. sorry about last week, I was . . . I don't know. we can talk. if you want.

God, do I want to talk to her?

I do. If only because she's one of the few links I have to Maggie, only because I might still have some sort of feeling for her and I don't even know her that well.

But I want to. I want to get to know her, not just because Maggie dated her.

yeah, sure. let's talk.

I press send without thinking, because I deserve to not think for once.

And then I turn my phone off.

I pull up to Julia's around six, her German shepherd, Gus, barking at my car. Julia runs out as I park, hair in a loose ponytail with tendrils falling around her face.

"We," she says as she runs up to my car, "are absolutely, totally, and completely out of junk food. Marisol's on a health kick and threw it all out, even Dad's hidden stash. Emergency run?"

"Oh my God, yes," I say.

She grins. "Good. Perfect. Let's go."

The gas station is about a mile from Julia's house. First time I spent the night with her she challenged me to a race there, and she beat me by a solid minute. I'm fast enough I can keep up with her now, but today we just walk, kicking at gravel with our beat-up tennis shoes.

"How was homecoming?" I ask her. "I never asked—did you and Chris . . . ?"

"No," she says, "I . . . I chickened out."

I wait for her tell me more, because the look on her face says she's going to, that she might.

"What did he say?"

"He was frustrated," she says, and she's twisting her braid

around fingers now. "Actually, Corey . . ."

"Hm?"

She lets out a breath. "I was just, like, looking up stuff, and I think . . . I don't know, maybe I'm asexual?"

The last few words come out in a rush so I barely understand her.

"It's this thing, like being bi, or gay, and it's where—you don't experience sexual attraction, or you might but only after you've known someone awhile, and . . ." She shrugs. "I don't know. It felt like it fits me, at least right now." She looks up at me, and she's close to tears. Silence stretches between us.

She came out to me. That's what's dimly registering in my mind right now, that my best friend just came out to me, before I had the courage to do the same thing with her.

"Oh," I say, and her face crumples and then I pull her into a tight hug. "Oh, Julie, I—I'm so glad you found a word that fits." I think of what Sneha said to me. "And I'm so glad you told me. That was—that was really fucking brave."

Julia relaxes as I hold her.

"Really?" she asks after a minute as we keep walking.

"Yeah," I say, and I squeeze her hand. "Yeah."

I could tell her. Right now. That that's how I felt when I realized I was bisexual, that finally having a word was such a relief. I could let her know she's not alone.

But I don't. Because she just came out to me, and I don't

want to make this about me, to do the same moments after she did.

We've worked up a sweat by the time we reach the gas station, grateful for the air-conditioning blasting even though it's starting to get cold outside.

"Okay, so I swiped twenty dollars from Mari's purse since she's the reason we're forced to do this, anyway," Julia says. "Come on."

The cashier doesn't even bother to look up from his phone. Julia heads straight for the Twizzlers and Swedish Fish; I grab a bag of chips and head to the freezer to grab ice cream for Julia. She's already at the front with the candy, including sour gummy worms that I hate the texture of. The cashier is eyeing her. Eyeing me.

This is not going to end well.

"Big plans for tonight?" he says, greasy hair falling over one eye.

It takes a minute before I realize he's talking to me. Or rather, talking *at* my boobs.

"Um. Yeah," I say, shoving the chips and ice cream toward him.

He nods. Grins. Still staring at my chest.

Julia reaches over below the counter, squeezes my hand.

He takes too long ringing up our chips, and when he's

handing back the change, he makes sure his hand brushes mine and I shudder.

"So . . . ," he says, turning to Julia. "Like. Uh. Do you speak English?"

Her eyes widen, her grip sharp on my hand. I watch as she reaches out and grabs our bags, not breaking eye contact with the cashier.

"Yeah," she says. "Fuck off."

She lets go of my hand and we run.

We make it back to her house and go up to her room, panting, sweaty like we've just finished practice.

"Fuck him," I say as soon as I flop on her bed and she shuts the door. "Like, seriously."

"No, don't want to," she says absentmindedly, and then she looks at me and we start cracking up, out of breath.

"It sucks that that happened though," I say. "Fuck."

Julia shrugs. "I get that all the time."

"You do?"

She stares at me then, hard. "I do," she says. "So does Chris. So do any of the other people of color in our school."

"I . . . I haven't noticed."

"No," she says. "You wouldn't."

I think then of things I've heard Trent say in the past. Not just saying he can't be racist because Chris is his best friend, but things like telling Julia talking about our periods was "fucking gross."

Maybe I have noticed. I've just ignored it because it's easier to fit in that way.

"I'm sorry I've never said anything," I say. "With—with Trent. With guys like that."

She sighs. "I know you said you don't notice that stuff, but . . . I need you to notice. It's really fucking hard to deal with that shit by myself and if you notice or say stuff, it keeps me from having to constantly do it. Because sometimes? Sometimes I'm just tired."

"Julie . . ."

"Like, I'm not going to tell you it's fine you haven't said anything, because it's not, but you're still my best friend," Julia says. She nudges my foot with hers. "Just try a little harder, okay?"

"Okay."

She nods.

"We should probably get to studying," she says, and cracks open a bag of Twizzlers and our chemistry textbook. But we're both breathing a little easier.

An hour later we're halfway through balancing chemical equations, one bag of Twizzlers, and a pint of ice cream. Julia asks me how to get iron oxide and carbon to form iron and carbon dioxide and I rattle it off in between bites of chips.

"How the hell does this make sense to you?" she asks. She's put her reading glasses on and is squinting down at the textbook.

"Because my dad's a computer geek and I have a head for numbers," I say as she tries to stump me with another equation. I stick another spoonful of ice cream in my mouth and try to talk through it. "Everyone thinks because I'm blond or a girl that I'm not good at science but they're wrong. I love science."

"And yet you hate bugs," Julia says, snickering.

"Bugs are disgusting. Put them under a microscope, that's one thing. Out in the wild?" I spread my arms out to show her just how much of the wild I'm encompassing. "No, thank you."

She laughs. "Do you think you'll study chemistry in college?"

"I don't know," I say. Maybe."

"Speaking of college . . ."

"Yeah, *great* segue—"

"How was Aldersgate? We haven't gotten to talk about it much."

I shrug and look down at my hands.

How *was* it?

I liked Sneha and Olivia. I liked hanging out, thought the party was okay. But that sense of wonder, of awe, of belonging I've heard the other girls talk about when they talk about college, all the things I feel like I'm supposed to feel?

Nothing.

"It was . . . good."

She waits a minute. "That's it?"

"I don't know what you want me to say," I say, and eat a few more chips to give myself time to think. "I mean, training was okay and they said they'd call, and I liked the girls on the team but . . . yeah. The party was better."

Julia turns around from the foot of the bed and stares at me. "You went to a party?"

Shit.

"I . . ."

"Nope. No backing out. Spill everything," she says, and she scoots herself farther up the bed until she's sitting next to me. She nudges my knee with hers. "Come on, Corey."

Julia almost never calls me Corey unless she wants something, so I know she's dying for me to spill. I lay my head back onto the pillow.

"The party was good. I don't remember much of it, to be honest," I say, shrugging, and Julia nails me with a glare, her dark eyebrows furrowed.

"Did you drink?"

"Not a lot."

"Enough to forget the party."

I shrug. "I guess."

She glares. "There's something you're not telling me."

"Juliaaaaa."

"You've been keeping secrets forever," she says accusingly,

and my face heats up because she's right, she's right. I keep lying to her because I'm terrified of telling her.

But maybe I should.

"I made out with someone," I mumble, and her eyes light up triumphantly.

"Someone who?" she asks.

"A short-haired someone."

"Was he cute?" she says, and I look away from her for a few seconds before she nudges my knee again. "Corey. He must've been seriously cute if you don't want to share with me. Either that or he was really super ugly."

say it say it say it say it—

"He . . . I didn't make out with a guy," I say, looking down at her comforter, debating shoving twenty Swedish Fish in my mouth.

"You made out with a *girl*?"

"Not so loud," I hiss. "But yes."

To my surprise, she frowns.

"So you're . . . so you're bi?" she asks.

I nod. "I mean—yes. I think so? No. Yes. I am. That's— that's how I identify, yeah. I'm bisexual."

Oh God I said it. I said the word. Out loud, and now I can see her remembering that time she laughed at Mr. Wilson's bisexual joke in Chem.

We just keep screwing up.

"How . . . how long have you known?"

"A while."

She nods. "Corey—why didn't you tell me? Did you think I wouldn't be cool with it or something?" There's a tinge of hurt at the edge of her voice.

"I was just scared," I say. And even now my heart is thumping like I've just finished running.

"You? Scared?"

I flinch.

"Shit, I'm sorry. Yeah, you're right. I was terrified to tell you I'm asexual, so—"

"I just didn't know how you'd react, and you're religious—"

Julia blinks. "Me being Catholic isn't going to stop me from being super accepting of you."

"I just thought—"

"No, yeah. I know what you thought. I live here too, you know," she says. And she squeezes my hand. "You know this doesn't change anything, right? You're still my best friend. I'm still going to have sleepovers and everything with you."

I nod. My throat is tight and a tear drips down my cheek and—no. I'm crying.

"Thanks, Julie," I say, and hug her, careful not to get tears on her shoulder.

"Plus," she says as we pull apart, "this means we can gossip about everyone you think is hot. Now. Tell me about who you made out with at the party. Is it super different from kissing a guy?"

I shrug. "Not super different. Just softer, I guess."

I could open up, tell her everything now—about Elissa, about Maggie, about who I am.

I could.

"So . . . ," I say, and my voice cracks when it comes out of my mouth and Julia looks at me. "Um. There's this girl I know. And I kinda kissed her but she won't talk to me much now but I think I like her and—"

"Tell. Me. Everything," Julia says, and the laugh that comes out of my mouth is high and strangled with relief.

God, I'm so glad this didn't change anything between us.

And I tell her about Elissa and I tell her about kissing her and how I can't stop thinking about her and I tell her and I tell her—

But I don't tell her about Maggie. About how I met Elissa. About the guilt eating me from the inside every time I think about kissing her. I am raw enough right now; I don't want to rip that wound open even further.

It's dark and I'm on the fuzzy edges of sleep when Julia speaks again.

"Hey, Corey?"

"Yeah?"

"How *did* you meet Elissa?"

She's not going to let me get away with this.

"I met her at a funeral."

I can hear rustling as Julia sits up. "No shit."

"Yeah."

"That's . . . wow."

"I know."

"Whose funeral?"

"You didn't know her," I say, immediately defensive because she can't know about Maggie. I want that piece of the story all to myself.

But Julia's smart, and I can see her piecing the puzzle together in her mind. "Corey . . ."

Don't say it.

Please don't put it together, I think, *oh please oh please.*

"That girl from Leesboro," Julia says slowly, and the name of Maggie's high school punches me straight in the gut. "You knew her, didn't you?"

"No—"

"Corinne."

"Yes," I whisper, and that admission nearly doubles me over. I jackknife on the air mattress, bring my knees to my chest.

"How did you know her?"

"It's not important," I say, voice raspy.

"It is, or you wouldn't be trying to hide it from me."

"Julia, please."

"You loved her," Julia says, shock in her voice. "Oh my God. Corey. That's why you reacted the way you did, that day— running out of the meet."

"Julia, no—"

"No. You did," she says, and her voice is certain. "You were in love with her. I didn't . . . I'm so sorry, Corinne," she says, and it's that sorry that gets me crying the hardest I have since I found out Maggie died, because I knew her, I know her, I loved her and I love her and I'm still not over her and I can't run from this anymore.

Julia gets down from the floor and heads over to me. "Hey, hey, it's okay. I'm sorry I brought it up."

"It's not okay," I say, sniffing, and she holds out the edge of her oversize T-shirt for me to blow my nose into.

"Do you want to talk about her?" Julia asks. "I mean . . . God, Corinne, how long have you been carrying this around?"

I can see her doing the mental math, calculating when we heard about Maggie's death. "One month," I say, quicker than she will, and the pity on her face just makes me want to cry more.

"How long were you dating?" she asks. "What was she like? Is it different dating a girl? Is she different from Elissa?" She makes a face. "Oh my God, you dated someone from Leesboro. You awful traitor," she says, laughing, but there's no malice in it.

"We dated for almost a year," I say. "She . . . she was wonderful. Really nice and she cared about everything and she loved to run and she wanted to teach." I think of Dylan's comments at the funeral. "And she had curly hair and it turned frizzy in the summer and she always smelled like strawberries and she kissed super well and she loved musicals even though she couldn't sing, and I loved a lot about her, Julie," I say. "I really, really did."

"Was it different? With her?"

"Than Trent?" I shrug. "Some things were the same. Some were completely different, and not just . . . not just that she was a girl. I had to hide it with Maggie, you know. And Elissa. I didn't have to do that with Trent."

Julia nods. "I know that's hard," she says, and it's nice to hear someone acknowledge it. "Is that why you've been pushing yourself?"

"Yeah."

"I wish you'd told me," she says, and I wish I had, too, but how could I?

"You won't tell anyone, will you?"

"Not unless you want me to," she says. "Are you going to come out?"

"I don't know. I don't think I'm brave enough."

"What're you afraid of, you think?" Julia pulls her hair over her shoulder and begins braiding it.

"Everything. You know what living here's like, Jules. Everyone knows everyone and everyone's business, and if you're a girl and you like girls . . ." I swallow. "You know how the girls on the team are. You're the only one I'm really close to, and I don't think the rest of them would react well. I just . . . I don't want it to backfire, you know? I don't want it to be some big, awful thing."

"I don't think it'll be as bad as you're thinking, Corinne," she says.

Everyone laughing in chemistry comes back to me again, Molly's comment from the night of the party. The way we gossip about the girls from other schools.

"If I come out, the whole school's going to see me as a slut who can't make up her mind," I say. "Or they'll think I'm gay because I dated a girl when I'm not. Or that I'm just doing it for attention."

Julia nods. "I didn't think about that. But hey. You'll figure it out. You're tough."

"Gee. That's comforting."

"You are. I know you don't think you are, but you are," she says. "You've been carrying all this around and you haven't cracked once, and I think that's tough as hell."

Is it stronger to crack, or not crack at all? On the inside I feel like I'm dying.

"Thanks."

"And hey," Julia says as she hoists herself back up onto her own bed. "Maybe you should talk to someone, you know? About Maggie. It can't be good keeping all that inside."

"I guess you're right."

"Like, I'm not saying you have to come out or anything, but you should at least tell your parents. Unless you think they'd kick you out or something."

"No, they wouldn't," I say. "Mom would probably be too drunk to even care, but Dad? I can't see him kicking me out for anything."

"I think you should try it," Julia says. "You know. If you're comfortable."

"Maybe."

I hear the covers shift as she rolls over onto her side. "And hey, Corinne?"

"Yeah?" I place my head on the pillow and pull the sleeping bag up under my chin.

"I'm sorry about your girlfriend," she says. "I really, am."

"Thanks, Julie," I mumble, and it's those words I fall asleep to.

I dream about Maggie.

We're running together, racing; our feet pounding the dirt in sync even though she's only one step ahead of me.

She's always one step ahead of me.

I open my mouth to call her name but nothing comes out and no matter how fast I run I can't catch up to her. We're running, running, running toward the finish line and I know she's going to cross it first but when she does—

She vanishes.

And when I cross the line, Elissa's waiting for me, and I kiss her and she kisses me back and then I hear something—

Booing. Everyone is booing. They're booing me and Elissa and Maggie and their cries roar in my ears until I wake up.

TWENTY-NINE DAYS G O N E.

Julia's mom makes us breakfast before Conference Championships. We still have school, still have to sit through classes.

I can't get that dream out of my head, though, and I have to make myself eat breakfast, grits and scrambled eggs. By the time we get to school my stomach is in knots, which it never is before a race, and I grip my backpack as Julia and I walk to our lockers.

Some of our teammates high-five us in the hallway. Seven of us get to go to Conference Championships. Seven of the best from each school in our district. If we place from there, we'll go to Regionals, and if we're lucky, State.

"You know Leesboro will be there too, right?" Julia says. "Even without—"

"Yeah," I say, just so I don't have to hear her say her name. "I know."

"You gonna be okay to run this course?"

I nod, tight smile. "Of *course* I am."

"That was a terrible pun," Julia says as we stop at her locker. Chris is already there, waiting, dressed in our team's colors and holding out a bunch of flowers for Julia, who squeals and wraps her arms around his neck.

Maggie's supposed to be there with me; I'm supposed to be sneaking off to the bathroom to call her to talk about Conference Championships and how excited I am to see her.

But she's not.

Chris spins Julia around and she catches my eye as he does, and I can't stand the fucking pity on her face.

So I turn away.

North Central Athletic Conference Championships are at Remington Park, out in Cary. Forty minutes on the bus there, forty minutes on the bus back. A few times heading down I-40 we pass the bus from Leesboro, and my breath catches before I remember she isn't going to be on it.

We pull up to the park around four. Our race isn't until four thirty so we mill around, stretch, scope out the competition from the other schools: Green Hill Catholic Prep, Raleigh Charter, Kestrel Heights. The boys from Kestrel eye us back, and we laugh and whisper behind our hands, watch as Haley, the bravest of us, goes up to one of them and gives him her number.

"Do you even know his name?" Addison asks her as she comes back, and I watch as Haley frowns for a split second before smiling again.

"Of course I do. Don't be ridiculous," she says. But she looks at me and rolls her eyes and I smile at her in solidarity, because I know what it's like to be a girl judged for who she's dating, who she flirts with.

Coach Reynolds gathers us into a group on the bleachers, and we jostle each other close, legs and knees and elbows bumping. We're a team. A perfect team with strong legs who've never made it to Conference before but are about to go out and kick some collective ass.

"I think it goes without saying how proud I am of how hard you've worked this semester," Coach Reynolds says. She makes eye contact with each of us, but it feels like she's staring at me the longest.

I get it. I've never run like this before, never showed any sort of motivation beyond keeping up with a certain girl from Leesboro, not that any of them would know that.

But here, now—if I can make it to State like she always wanted to, then maybe . . .

What?

Maybe I can bring her back.

Coach Reynolds goes on to talk about how we've inspired her and how proud she is of her team, and how even if we don't win today she'll still be proud, all the typical coach stuff she saves for meet days.

Julia looks over toward the end of her speech, squeezes my hand.

We're going to do this.

I am running. I only have a vague idea where I am in the group but I can hear my sneakers hitting the ground and feel my arms pumping through the air and the breeze as another girl passes me, the ache in my muscles because of how I'm pushing myself.

Run faster run harder be better.

It's her voice in my head saying it so I do, passing a girl from Green Hill Catholic who shoots me a look as I nearly elbow her.

I have to win, though. I have to win this.

I round a corner, nearly trip over an exposed tree root but catch myself before I go down.

I can't fall now. Can't trip up, because I have to catch up to Maggie.

I run harder. Run faster. Pass Julia, pass Haley.

They want *this*, the race, the feeling of winning.

I just want my girlfriend back.

I come in third, first on our team. I'm not sure how it happens— one minute I'm running, the next I'm crossing the finish line and Coach Reynolds is standing there cheering and in the crowd I see my Dad and then, farther away, I see—

Elissa?

What's she doing here?

Coach Reynolds pats me on the back and tells me she's been so impressed with me lately, and my dad is in the stands grinning and polishing his glasses and I'm still, always, looking for a girl.

I break away from my coach, give a wave to my dad, don't stop to stretch even though I probably should, and head over to the spot behind the bleachers I'm certain Elissa is at.

It's her. Baseball cap pulled over her curls, dark green army jacket, baggy pants. Hands fiddling with her phone, chipping navy polish on light brown skin.

"Elissa?"

She turns, and her face is sharp and beautiful and I'm remembering what it was like to kiss her—

And then I remember my dream, and it's all I can do to keep from shuddering.

"Hi," she says.

"What are you doing here?"

She shrugs. "Came to watch you. You said you wanted to talk, so . . . I'm here."

"That's . . ."

But I don't know what it is. "How'd you know where it was?"

"Dylan and I used to—we used to come watch Maggie," she says. "They don't change the location of these meets, you know, and I figured . . . we could talk. We should talk," she adds.

"Okay. So talk."

She nods. Swallows.

Hypothesis: I could kiss her. Here. Right now. I could apologize and I could kiss her and the world would

stop.

"Look," she says. "I'm sorry about how I reacted. With everything. But losing . . . losing Maggie has been hard and you've just made it harder and I—I don't know how to handle it or how I feel about you but I shouldn't have—"

"Shouldn't have what?"

"I shouldn't have pushed you away," she says, and my breath catches in my throat. "Look, I know this is hard and I know we're both still—still grieving, but I . . ."

She kisses me. She leans in and kisses me under these bleachers where anyone could see us if they looked hard enough and her mouth is firm against mine and my body is still full of adrenaline from this race and from her lips *and*—

I pull back.

"We could give this a shot," I say, and I look at her. There's no Maggie here, no ghost. It's just me and a girl I like under the bleachers, such a cliché.

"Okay, yeah," she says. "Okay."

Julia's staring at me as we walk to the bus. The rest of our teammates are ahead, chanting some cheer from one of our football games and screaming, because we're going to Regionals.

"Where'd you disappear to after the race?" Julia asks as we lag behind. "We couldn't find you."

I open my mouth to lie and hate that it's become instinct. I swallow it down. "Elissa came to the meet."

"And?"

"And I kissed her," I say.

"You *didn't*," she says.

"I did," I say, and Julia reaches over and grips my hand.

"Tell me everything later," she says, and I can't stop the grin from spreading over my face because for the first time I have someone to tell everything to later.

The bus back is raucous. Noisy. We're cheering and shrieking and singing along to pop songs and it smells like sweat and floral perfume and deodorant, like victory. There's no denying it. We're going to Regionals; Coach just needs to figure out who she wants to nominate.

Julia's sitting next to me and texting Chris. "He wants me to come over and celebrate," she says, and her face is flushed, eyes bright. She looks at me. "Should I? I . . . I guess it'd be a good time to come out to him."

"Do you want to?"

She thinks about it. "Not yet. I want to go home and take a bath and watch *Vampire Diaries*."

"Then do that. He'll understand," I say, and she nods and texts him.

Someone pulls a speaker out of her backpack. Someone else turns the music to Carly Rae Jepsen. Julia grabs my hand and uses it as a microphone, singing loudly along with the rest of the team.

And in this moment, I genuinely belong with these girls. I'm not faking my way through it, not laughing at jokes I don't get just so I can fit in. I belong here. I belong on this bus next to Julia while we sing Carly Rae Jepsen in really awful voices; I belong on this cross-country team.

I belong, I belong, I belong.

ONE MONTH G O N E.

The next day Coach calls me into her office, just minutes before practice starts. My first thought is that I'm in trouble, that she's somehow found out about Maggie. It's not against the rules to date our rivals, it's not against the rules to date a girl, and yet somehow I'm afraid if she finds out she'll kick me off the team, or she'll realize I'm an imposter.

"Have a seat, Corinne," she says, smiling at me. Coach Reynolds's face is weathered and sun-beaten, white skin slightly wrinkled and tan from spending time outside. She has laugh lines around her eyes. I want to look like that when I get older. I want to laugh enough to have permanent marks on my face from it.

She's been Ridgeway's coach since 2017, pulling our team out of a losing streak, yet we've never been good enough to be better than okay. I wonder if that frustrates her.

I wonder what it's like to care that much.

"How's senior year treating you?" she asks, looking across her desk at me.

"It's all right," I say. "Kind of a blur, to be honest."

Coach smiles. "I bet. How many times have you been told it's the best year of your life?"

"More than I can count," I say.

"Mm. Don't listen to that. College is better," she says, and laughs. I don't really know what to say to that. Most of the adults around here keep insisting that I'm going to miss high school *so much* when I'm gone, and how they wish they could go back and relive it.

"Did you just call me in here to talk about high school?" I ask, then immediately regret how bitchy it sounds.

"I didn't," Coach says. "I wanted to talk about Regionals."

A lump forms in my throat. "What about them?"

"I have to have my nominations in in two days," she says. "And I'm nominating you this year."

I can't believe what I'm hearing. I look down at my hands, clenched into fists, the watchband tan on my arm. I tell myself to relax, but it doesn't work.

"Why?" I ask.

Coach laughs again. "Because you've been running so well. I'm impressed. Your times are up, your stamina's improving— quite frankly, Corinne, I've never seen you run like this before."

Don't ask me why, I think. *Please don't ask me why.*

"Guess I'm just trying to put more effort in. Since it is senior year," I say, but it sounds hollow even to me.

Coach nods. "I've had a few schools call about you."

"You have?"

"Mm. Want me to write them down? You can give the coaches a call."

My head is spinning.

This is what I wanted, right? This is how I get out of here— by running as fast as I can. This is how I get to a good school, pack my bags, leave town. I run.

"Sure," I say. "Yeah, that'd be great."

"Wonderful." Coach fishes some paper and a pen out of her desk and begins scribbling on it.

"Who else are you nominating?" I ask. "For Regionals, I mean."

I know seven of us get to go.

Coach purses her lips. "I'm not supposed to reveal that until later." But then she winks at me. "But Julia's going, if that's what you're asking."

I beam. "It is. Thank you."

But for the first time, I find myself thinking about Haley. Whether she's going to Regionals, whether she gets to. Whether she wants to.

"Has she made a decision on colleges yet? You two going somewhere together?"

Shame burns in my chest because it's never crossed my mind to go to college with Julia.

"I don't know. I think she's trying to coordinate with Chris," I say, and Coach nods.

"Makes sense. Go change, okay? You can tell Julia about Regionals, but don't tell the rest of your teammates just yet; I'll announce after practice today."

"Okay," I say. I stand, hoist my bags over my shoulder.

"I'm proud of you, Parker," Coach says as I leave her office, and those are the words that carry me into the locker room.

TWO MONTHS BEFORE.

This is Maggie, spreading out her plan for us.

For her.

She lays all the brochures on her bed, color coded with sticky notes. Blue for safety schools, green for reach schools, yellow for dream schools that will probably still call her because she's just that good. Pink sticky notes are included on a few brochures.

Those are Corinne schools. Schools I like, schools I would go to with her. Clemson, Aldersgate, Jefferson, Villanova, Florida State.

I watch as she arranges them all on her bed, pulls up a spreadsheet on her laptop and begins typing stats, like average GPA and SAT score and whether they're Division I and how fast we need to be next year for them to let us in.

I don't know if I want to be let in.

I watch as she adds another tab, one that mentions if the school is near a city, has an LGBTQ center, if it's still in the South, if it seems generally accepting.

My stomach sinks further.

"So what do you think?" she asks.

I pick up a blue brochure. Aldersgate College. My dad's school. Watch the slight frown form on her face, watch it disappear as my knee brushes hers.

Do I tell her I'm destined to go here? I'm not like her; I don't have big dreams? That she may want big city life and Division I but I—

I set the brochure down. And when she picks up a Villanova brochure—yellow and pink sticky notes on this one—I smile.

THIRTY-THREE DAYS G O N E.

My life is a whirlwind. Between meeting up with Elissa (secretly), running my heart out at practice, and work, I am on fire.

I spend my nights alternating between scrolling through Maggie's Instagram and calling Elissa just so I can hear her voice. It's become routine, to fall asleep with that rasp in my ear. We talk about everything. Anything. I haven't been this open with anyone except Maggie, and I don't know if the fact it's over the phone makes it any different, but I ask her things I'd never ask anyone else.

Sometimes we talk about Maggie. Mostly we don't; mostly we avoid the subject.

"What was it like? Dating her?" I ask. It's two a.m. and I'm lying on my side, knees to my chest, phone to my ear.

"I don't know why you want to know about that," Elissa says.

Because I want to know what she was like with you. What you were like with her. If it was different.

And if I know how Maggie was with Elissa, how they acted together, then it'll be like she's here.

Won't it?

"Just tell me."

"Corinne . . ."

"*Please,*" I say. "I want to know."

She sighs. I can hear her shift over the phone. And just when I think she isn't, just when I think she's going to fall asleep and not tell me, she does.

"It was . . . I dunno. It was nice. We dated for four months, but then we just kinda broke it off because it wasn't working."

"Oh. Were you . . . were you out?"

"To a few people, yeah," she says.

Maggie's voice comes into my head, all the times she asked me about coming out.

But I don't want to think about Maggie right now. About how Elissa was braver than I was.

I want to be brave. Just once. "So . . . ," I say. "There's going to be a Halloween party after our Regionals meet at Haley's house—well, okay, in her barn. Do you . . ." My mouth is dry. "Would you maybe wanna go?"

"With you?" she says.

I know what she means. What she's asking. "Yes. With me."

There's silence on the other end of the line, silence that stretches on for so long I'm afraid she's hung up.

"Corinne, are you sure?"

I pause.

What would it be like? To be out with her, to hold her hand as we walk down the street, to do all the things with her that I never did with Maggie.

Could I do it?

Am I brave enough to do it?

"I . . . It's just a party."

But it's more than that, and we both know it.

"Are you sure you want to, though? We don't have to," Elissa says. "I don't . . . I don't want to pressure you. Or make this difficult."

"You're not. And I'm the one asking you, remember? I just . . . I don't want a big statement or anything, but Regionals is a big deal, and I want you to come to this party with me. Please?"

It's the same please Maggie used when we'd fight about this because there are a thousand words in that please, a thousand questions.

Why don't you love me?

Why don't you want to be out with me?

Are you ashamed of me?

Are you scared?

Are you?

Are you?

"Okay," she says. "Okay."

FIVE MONTHS BEFORE.

Late at night, I scroll through blogs on a private browser on my phone. I search *coming out*.

What would it be like if I did? If I could, if I wanted to?

I read everyone's stories until they echo in my head, until I feel like they're my own.

my mom totally accepted me

my mom hated me

my stepmom kicked me out

I'm living on the street

help me someone help me

I thought it would make everything better

it did make everything better

my whole family knows

my mom said it was just a phase

what if it's just a phase

my dad said I was too young to know how I feel

I live with my granddad he's a WWII vet you know

what he said? he said he didn't care. he said he loved
me anyway
my girlfriend wants me to come out
my partner asked me not to
I've never even kissed anyone how am I supposed to
know if I'm gay?
they won't let me use the right bathroom at school
they all said they love me anyway
is it worth it?
it was totally worth it I'm so much happier
I wish I'd just stayed in the closet

God.

I don't know what to do. I don't know if I want everyone to know.

I want to be proud of Maggie. I want to be proud of us, I want her to be proud of me.

But where we live, who we are—is it better to stay in the closet?

Is it easier?

I don't know.

THIRTY-NINE DAYS G O N E.

Trent catches me in the hallway the day before Regionals, coming up to my locker with a pink flower in his hand.

"Hey," he says, as I'm trying not to let my chemistry textbook topple me over.

"Hey," I say, looking at him, brown eyes and pale freckled skin and easy smile. It's easy to remember why I liked him, easy to remember just how simple things were with Trent. Not bad simple, just . . . simple.

"What's the flower for?" I ask, gesturing to it.

"You, I guess," he says. "For Regionals tomorrow."

"Oh." I say. "I . . . thanks."

"You're going to be great," he says. "Really."

"Thanks," I say again, and I mean it this time.

We fall into step beside each other, walking to AP English. I'm reminded of last year, of my life with Trent.

He flashes me that smile I got so used to seeing, but there's no twinge in my gut like before, just a comfort at having him next to me.

"So, you dating anyone?" I ask, easy.

He laughs. "Naw. Not yet. Might take Haley to winter formal, though. She's real cute."

"She is," I say.

"You should take her, then," he says.

I stop in the hall. Someone nearly runs into my backpack.

Does he know does he know does he—

But when I dare to face him, he's smiling. Joking.

"Ha, ha," I say dryly. "Maybe I will."

He frowns a little. "I was kidding, you know."

"No, I know. But why would it be a joke—if I took her?"

He shakes his head. "Forget it."

But I don't want to forget it; I want to push him, ask what he meant.

But that's not the girl I was with him. It's not who I am.

We enter the classroom in silence, and Trent heads to his normal seat at the back.

"Thanks for the flower," I say, but he doesn't acknowledge me at all.

Haley looks at it, then back at Trent, back at me.

"Y'all dating again?" she asks, and I can hear a note of jealousy in her voice.

"No," I say. Then I pick the flower up from my desk, hand

it to her. "You can have it."

She smiles and tucks it behind her ear. Trent was right. She is cute. Ambitious and cute, and I wonder why I hated her before.

I sit next to Haley in Calculus, surreptitiously texting while she takes notes and Mr. Oshetskie tries to drill holes in my forehead with his eyes.

Mr. Osh. Our ancient math teacher. No one likes him. Boys call him "O-shit-skie" under their breath. Girls whisper that he'll stare at your chest if you go up to the desk to ask for help, that if you're staying after to ask a question then don't wear a short skirt or low-cut shirt, and sit as far from him as you can.

Like lack of a short skirt stops men like Mr. Osh. He's been teaching here longer than our principal has worked here. He remembers when students hid under their desks because of threat of a nuclear bomb, when girls all wore dresses and he was young and attractive enough that he was "charming" and "dangerous" instead of a pervert.

I hide my phone under the desk and text Elissa. Ask again if she's sure she wants to come to the party with me, and do we just want to meet there or what?

But before I can see her response, a shadow falls over my desk. Osh.

"Miss Parker," he says, "is there something more interesting on your phone than the wonders of parabolas?"

"No, sir," I say, and flash him my best smile, the one saved for teachers and creeps who stare when I run around my neighborhood sometimes, the one that says *I don't like you/I'm afraid of you but if I don't smile then you'll—*

"Then you'll have no problem if I take it, then," he says, and before I know anything his sweaty palm has slapped onto my desk and he's leaning over me, waiting for me to whine or bitch or give him the satisfaction of seeing me squirm.

I don't do any of those things. I look straight ahead like he isn't there and I slide my phone into his hand and try not to grimace. Everyone is looking at me. Even Haley looks sympathetic.

"You can get your phone back after class," he says, and I want to bury my face in my hands but instead I just roll my eyes like it doesn't bother me, and he goes back to teaching and I go back to taking notes.

Haley nudges me with her elbow. "You okay?" she whispers.

"Yeah, I'm fine," I say.

"Osh is a dick."

"Yeah, he is," I say.

"I'll stay with you when you get your phone after class—if you want," she says.

I stare at her. "Yeah. Thanks," I say, and she grins, ducking her head.

She passes me notes through the rest of class, and somehow, that makes it better.

Julia bumps into me in the hallway after class, reaching out and squeezing my shoulder.

"What's up?"

"Osh took my phone," I say, stuffing it back in my bag, wiping my hands on my jeans.

"Yikes. Everything ok?"

"Yeah, Haley waited for me while I got it back," I say.

"Didn't know you two were becoming so close," Julia says, surprise on her face as we walk down the hall toward her locker.

I shrug. "Occupational hazard, I guess. You going to her party tomorrow night?"

"Mm, no," Julia says. "Why? Are you?"

"I might."

"Trent going?"

"I have no freaking clue," I say. "And he likes Haley anyway, so."

"I know, but I saw him with that flower by your locker today, so I thought—"

I cut her off. "We're not back together."

"People are going to talk like you are," she says, and as if on cue two freshman girls giggle behind their hands when they see me.

What would they do if they knew I liked girls, too?

"Elissa going?" Julia asks, voice muffled as she holds her

ponytail holder in her mouth and pulls her hair back.

God, can the whole school hear her asking me that?

"I dunno."

"Did you ask her?"

"Yeah."

"And?"

"Can we talk about this later, Julie?" I ask. "It's just a party. It's not a big deal. She's coming with me; there's nothing to talk about."

"Corinne."

"Seriously," I say, looking at her. "She's just coming to the party with me. That's it."

We know that's not just it.

She touches my arm. "I just want to make sure you're happy, Corey. And that you're doing what you want."

"I am."

"Good," she says, and she looks like she might say more, but my phone buzzes and it's Elissa, and I shield it with my hands and walk away before Julia can read the message.

I'm sure. Are you?

My hands shake.

I'm not sure. I have no idea what I want anymore.

Yeah, I reply. **I am.**

FORTY DAYS G O N E.

I wake up with my heart hammering like I've already run. *Regionals Regionals Regionals* pounds out a steady rhythm in my breast.

But then a louder one comes along. Stronger.

Come out come out come out come out come out—

I don't know if I can.

Come out come out come out come out

I pull my covers over my head, forget about Regionals and coming out for just five more blissful minutes.

Julia's knee touches mine the entire ride to Regionals.

My phone buzzes in my pocket the entire time.

I ignore both of them.

Our race is at Gateway Park. Five thousand meters over a trail with twists and turns none of us have ever run.

There's no pep talk from Coach this time. Nothing except steely-eyed determination.

She wants us to win. We've never made it here before, so now we have to win. We all have something to prove.

They give us our numbers and we line up at the starting line, hair pulled tight, muscles ready.

I catch a glimpse of the girls from Leesboro all the way on the other side of the line. My hand goes to Maggie's scrunchie in my hair. It's absurd to think they'll recognize it, to think they'll care, but I can't help myself.

Part of me wants them to recognize it. Part of me wants a girl to storm up to me and demand to know why I'm wearing her captain's hair scrunchie.

I'll say it's because we were dating.

I'll say it's for luck.

And then I'll run away.

The starting gun goes off and my legs run without me thinking and I shouldn't be using this much energy now I should be saving it for the end of the race or I'm going to burn myself out but all I can think with each thud of my spikes is—

Come out come out come out

She should be here. She wanted this, she wanted to be invited, and I—I just wanted whatever she wanted.

I push myself harder.

I'm doing this for her, but I—I don't know if I want this

because she did or because I actually want it.

I can't think about that now. I need to focus, focus on the trees ahead of me and my feet touching the ground and pushing myself to go harder, faster, to win win win—

come out come out come out—

I cross the finish line, unaware of anything except my team cheering and people screaming my name and my school's name and the sweat on my forehead, my neck.

My hands reach up, touch Maggie's scrunchie, and I look at the scoreboard.

Seventeen minutes. For a 5K. It's a PR for me, a win possibly for our school if Haley and Julia and the other four girls keep this up.

But I did that. Me. I ran that fast; I helped our team get that far.

And for this moment I've crossed the finish line with air in my lungs and Maggie's scrunchie in my hair, I am the one who wants this.

We celebrate on the bus back to school. We won. We're going to State.

Haley and Julia and Alicia came in seventh, twelfth, and nineteenth. So we're going.

None of us has ever made it this far.

And right now, we're a team. We are sweat and sore legs and

stretches on the way back and athletic tape and laughter, thumps on the back and "Holy shit, girl, you ran hard out there."

That last comment is directed at me. But it's not said with the pride it was at Conference. It's said with disbelief, whispered looks, and glances my way.

I am not a girl who pushes herself. I am a girl who stays in the middle and doesn't draw attention, and now that I'm getting better, now that I don't fit, they don't know what to do with me.

I want them to be proud of me, my team. For the first time I actually want them to be proud of me, and maybe they are. Or will be.

I hug my knees to my chest even though they'll probably cramp later. There's a text on my phone waiting from Elissa, about Haley's party.

Speaking of.

"Party at my place tonight!" Haley shouts, and the whole bus cheers. "Halloween party, obviously, but you don't have to dress up if you don't want."

We cheer again. No one likes dressing up anymore. Half the school shows up as football players or cheerleaders anyway, so it doesn't feel special, not like when we were kids.

"You going to the party?" Julia asks once everyone's quieted down.

"I told you I am."

"With Elissa?"

I shoot her a look, a *can-we-not-talk-about-this-on-the-bus* look. She ignores it and leans closer to me, takes my phone.

You said we'd talk later. It's later. Talk, she types.

I take my phone back from her, stuff it in my pocket. "No."

"Are you okay?"

"I'm fine, Jules."

"You sure? With the way you ran back there . . ."

"What?" I snap. "You wanted me to be better, didn't you? Isn't that what everyone wanted, me to improve? I'm improving."

"Yeah, but is that what *you* want?" she asks.

I don't answer her, and after a minute she sighs and changes the subject. "Seriously. Are you worried about tonight?"

"Why would I be worried?"

Julia frowns. *"Corinne."*

"Sorry."

"You don't have to go if you don't want to," she says. "Or I'll ditch Chris and come with you. Safety net and all. Or I can wait at your mom's, and you can come back and tell me if anything happens."

"I don't want you at the party if—if people react badly," I say. I kick at the seat in front of me. "And it's not like you'd want to stay with my mom alone." I sigh. "I shouldn't be doing this."

"Coming out if you're not ready? No, you shouldn't be."

"Whose side are you on?"

"Yours," she says. "Always."

We shouldn't be having this conversation on the bus, but I can't stop myself. "I'm scared."

"Then don't do it. You don't have to come out if you don't want to, Corinne," she says.

But I feel like I have to. It's unfair to Elissa if I don't—and it is, I know it is. It was unfair to Maggie that I wouldn't.

Here is what I never told Maggie: I am terrified down to the bone of what everyone else will think of me. I do not make waves. I keep my head down and keep running forward and ignore what everyone else says, but sometimes I can't. I tell myself I wouldn't give a damn if they knew about me, but I would. I would.

I do.

I text Elissa Haley's address and tell her I'll meet her there, hands shaking as I do so.

It's just a party. I've been to a lot of parties. I'll be fine.

Mom cooks dinner, just the two of us since Brett's out refereeing a game. Every so often the doorbell will ring, and she'll get up and put on a witch's hat and hand out candy to kids, while I sit at the table and try not to be seen.

"Do you remember," she says when she comes back to sit down, "the year you dressed up as a mermaid for Halloween and begged me to put blue streaks in your hair?"

"And then I went swimming at a party the next day and they all turned out green? Yeah, I remember," I say, and she smiles.

"I think I have a picture of that, still," she says. "Somewhere."

She taps her nails on a glass, head down. It's just water, but it still makes me nervous.

"You call me if you need me to get you from the party, okay?" she says. "I know you're staying with Julia, but if you need me . . ."

If I call her it's not likely she'll be able to come get me, anyway.

"Yeah, okay," I say, and look away so I don't have to see her face fall.

Maybe I should just stay home with her.

"You can eat all the leftover candy," she says, and I smile. She suddenly reaches over and squeezes my hand, opens her mouth like she's about to say something.

I could tell her. Here. Now. I could tell her I'm going to this party with a girl and I'm scared out of my mind, I could tell her how I ran today, how I keep running because the girl I loved wanted me to and I don't know how to stop.

But instead, I push back from the table and go get ready for the party, and she goes to the fridge and grabs a bottle of wine and we don't say anything to each other that we should.

. . .

I can hear the music thumping through Haley's barn before I've even stepped out of my car. Everyone's milling about, cups in hands, no masks tonight—there's no need to hide here. It's Halloween. We can be wild, crazy teenagers, unveil our true selves.

My hair hangs straight down past my shoulders, a blond curtain. My eyeliner is bright blue and precise; I'm in tight black jeans and shimmery silver top.

I am perfect. I am unstoppable. For a second, I am the girl I was with Trent, *so pretty so popular don't you want to be her?*

And then I spot Elissa, and my bravado fades. She's leaning against the barn and has her hands shoved in her pockets, curly hair jammed under a snapback, shoulders hunched under a denim jacket.

You can tell by looking at her.

You can tell you can tell you can tell she's—

I swallow.

"Hey," I call, and I hope my voice doesn't get carried away by the noise of the party, but her head snaps up, and she grins.

I am the cause of that grin, and butterflies start in my stomach.

"Hey, yourself," she says. Her hands fidget at her pockets. She smells like smoke.

"Thanks for coming," I say, at the same time she says, "You look—"

We laugh nervously, stop.

"How do I look?" I ask.

"Amazing," she says.

She doesn't try to lean in and kiss me, and I'm grateful. Even though I want her to.

God, can I do this? Can we do this? Am I brave enough to go into this party with her, brave enough to be out with her in a way Maggie and I weren't?

Elissa must sense my hesitation, because she stops just outside Haley's barn. "Corinne, we don't have to do this," she says. "If you're scared."

"What would we do instead?" I ask, voice low.

"I have an idea," she says.

I shiver, and not from the cold. Reach down, wind my fingers through her own. We are two girls standing in the dark near the entrance to Haley's barn. We know what this means.

But Elissa's right. I'm not ready to go into that party, not ready to face everyone with this girl.

"Want to get out of here?" she says, lips brushing my ear. I shiver.

"Yeah. Okay," I say, and she takes my hand and we leave.

We drive back to her place separately, me following her so I don't leave my car at Haley's barn and have everyone ask where I am, who I'm with.

My heart pounds the entire time. I keep the radio off.

Do I want to do this?

I pull up in front of her house, put my car in park, and take my keys out of the ignition, shaking hands nearly dropping them. Watch as she gets out of her truck and comes over to my car, waiting for me.

I get out, and she looks at me. Smiles, almost nervously. We both know what this is going to lead to, we both know what we're hurtling toward, and yet neither of us is doing anything to stop it.

I don't think we want to stop it.

Elissa steps toward me, so close I could reach out and pull her to me, if I was brave enough.

"Want to go inside?" she asks, and I swallow.

"Won't your roommate hear us?"

Elissa turns to look at me. "No. She's out for the night."

"Oh."

We stop on her front porch, and she looks at me, hard. "Corinne," she says. "We don't . . . we don't have to do this if you're not ready. You can go home, or back to the party, or . . . or wherever. I won't mind."

I don't answer. I reach up and pull her face down to mine and I kiss her, hard, like that first time in her truck. She doesn't pull away this time, and neither do I, and then she's laughing and unlocking the doors and we're practically running inside.

She's barely shut the door when she gently pushes me against the wall, her hands at my waist, kissing my neck. I tangle my hands in her hair and pull her mouth up to mine, kiss her like my life depends on it. She tugs at the hem of my shirt and pulls it over my head, briefly breaking our kissing. When she moans, I move my lips to her neck and my hands to the zipper on her jeans.

"Corinne . . . Corinne, wait," she says, and she pulls back from me. I groan.

"What?"

"I just . . . I . . . Do you want to do this?"

"Do what?" I ask.

She waves her hands in between us, indicates the fact that I'm shirtless. "This. Us. Tonight, whatever. I don't . . ."

"I don't know," I say. "I just . . . God, Elissa, I don't want to think about it. I don't want to think about what this means or what it has to mean or—or—"

Maggie's name is on my lips but if I say it this isn't happening.

We are so close we could touch. Kiss. Nose to nose, hip to hip.

What's stopping us?

What's stopping me?

Don't I want this? Don't I want to be with her?

I have always been a girl who goes along with what everyone else wants. Who keeps her mouth shut and her opinions and needs and wants tucked inside where no one can get to them.

But this, tonight—I want her. No complications, no messiness, no thinking. Just hands and lips and skin.

But how do I let her in? Maggie took what was left of my heart with her, shattered in pieces on I-85. I've kept the remnants guarded in my chest in their cage, but Elissa . . .

"Yes," I say. "I want this. I want *you*."

Her lips meet mine, then, and I understand. She's not asking for love, not asking to make me whole again, and I'm not asking her to. We're not asking each other to forget.

We're just asking for one night together.

She still tastes like cigarettes, but she smells like cloves and vanilla, and we are kissing, kissing, and she's guiding me so my back is against the armrest of the couch and her thigh is between my legs and suddenly I want so, so much more than kissing.

I gasp her name and we move so I'm lying on the couch and she is on top of me and we're pulling at each other's clothing and her lips are on my neck and she reaches behind me and undoes my bra, tosses it on the floor, laughing while she does. Then her hands are back on me and she's touching me like I do myself and God, God, I want this I want this I want this.

She pulls my jeans down and reaches for the waistband of my underwear and she looks at me, lips swollen and eyes bright.

"Is this okay?" she asks.

I nod, and she pulls them down and then her mouth is on me and my hands in her hair and I want this I want this I want her *I want*—

FORTY-ONE DAYS G O N E.

I wake up the next morning in another girl's bed.

I don't know where I am.

But then I look over and see Elissa's sleeping form next to me and her curls splayed out on the pillow and—

I kissed her. I had sex with her. The world didn't end.

She stirs. Rolls, looks over at me with a sleepy smile. "Hey," she says, her voice low. "You just get up?"

"Yeah." I bend down, suddenly shy, fumble on the floor for my clothes.

"Want some coffee or something?"

"What time is it?"

She groans. "Ten. Why?"

"I should probably head back. I told my mom I was staying with Julia, and . . ."

"No, yeah, I get it," Elissa says. Then she reaches over, grabs my hand. "You okay?"

"Why wouldn't I be?" I ask, pulling away and standing up and shimmying back into my jeans.

"Yeah, you're right," she says.

But I still turn my back to her to pull my shirt over my head.

"I'll call you, okay?" I say, wince at how cliché that sounds coming out of my mouth. "I mean . . ."

"I get it," she says. "Look, Corinne . . . it's okay. We're okay. Last night was great. We can talk about it later—we don't have to put a label on anything right now."

"Yeah, I know," I say, turning back to her. I bend down, kiss her, long and slow.

"Just think about it?" she says, and she smiles.

And I put the rest of my clothes on and try not to hurry out of her house.

My head is buzzing on the drive to my mother's. Buzzing with thoughts of Elissa and her hands and lips on me and Regionals and running and *come out come out come out*.

Could I?

Last night with Elissa was . . . I don't know.

But could I do it? Come out? Be out, where everyone knows, where everyone looks at me and sees a girl who dates girls and boys?

Or will they see me as a slut, as a girl doing it for attention, as—

But I am getting tired of hiding.

I could start small. I don't have to make a big declaration, a parade, turn it into anything. I told Julia. I could tell someone else. I could maybe tell my mother, maybe.

I could do it.

I'm going to do it.

My car rumbles as I pull into my mother's driveway. My hair is in a messy ponytail. I'm in last night's clothes because I went home with a girl and I am going to come out to my mother.

I can do this.

I get my keys out of my pockets, prop open the screen door with my hip, and unlock the door.

The house is a mess. I almost trip over one of the dogs when I come in. There are dishes in the sink and clothes everywhere and dishes on the table and bottles and my mother is—

Asleep. On the couch. Also in her clothes from yesterday.

God, how can I come out? How can I tell her now when she won't even remember?

Dad wants me to get away from here, wants me to escape this town and this life, but how can I leave Mom? How can I leave when she's like this? When I'm not here to visit her on weekends and make sure she doesn't drink too much, when I'm not here to tell whatever latest boyfriend that she's like this, because if I don't take care of her, if I'm not around to check on her—

Who will?

...

She is not my responsibility, I tell myself on the drive home. My mother is not my responsibility. I am not the one who is supposed to check on her, to take care of her.

Then why do I feel like she is?

FORTY-TWO DAYS G O N E.

I leave for school as early as I can the next morning, cutting out before Dad is even awake. My heart thrums in my chest, muscle memory at the acrobatics it did when Elissa touched me.

Come out come out come out.

I shove the thought away.

At lunch I sit with ChrisandTrentandJuliaandHaley, now that Haley and Trent are dating. Apparently, he asked her out at her party, and if you believe Marianna Wheeler's gossip, they spent the rest of the evening making out in the bathroom, his truck still in her driveway long after everyone else had left.

She's smiling secretly and he's looking at her and I know he's holding her hand under the table and I'm just glad they're both happy.

But now I'm the odd one out, the literal fifth wheel in this group.

Julia nudges me with her foot. "How was the party?" she asks quietly.

Her timing is perfect. "Yeah," Haley pipes up. "You were there for like what, two seconds? Who were you with? I barely saw you."

"What'd you guys do?" I ask, choosing to ignore their questions and turning instead to Chris, who shrugs.

"Just went to Raleigh and caught a movie," he says.

"Which movie?"

"You're avoiding the question," Haley says.

"Yeah, what were you doing at that party?" Trent asks.

"Shit, I forgot the name. But it was about this artist who was color-blind—" Chris starts.

"Chris, don't answer, she's stalling," Trent says. "Anyway—wait, why'd you go see *that*?"

"Because I wanted to?"

"Dude, that's—"

"It's *what*?" I snap, my voice too loud. TrentandHaleyand-ChrisandJulia look at me. "I mean if Chris goes to see a movie about an artist, what does that mean?"

Trent shrugs. "You know," he says.

"No, I don't."

"Why are you being such a bitch?" he asks, and my face and temper flares.

Haley drops his hand. But she doesn't sit there quietly like I would have, doesn't look around the table in disbelief. Instead, she stands up with her cafeteria tray in her hand while Trent gawks at her.

"What?"

"You don't get to call Corinne a bitch, Trent. *Also* it shouldn't matter what movie Chris sees, *also* you're being a real ass right now, so I'm going to walk away, and if you want to keep dating me, you're going to learn to think twice about the things that come out of your mouth," she says, and walks off.

Chris whistles. Julia smiles. Trent sulks and looks at me like he expects me to back him up.

I can feel Julia looking at me.

"She's right," I say. "You shouldn't have called me a bitch, and it doesn't matter what movie Chris went to see."

"You're just saying that so we don't ask you about the party," he says, and I look up at him.

"I'm saying it because you're being an asshole."

"You didn't think I was an ass before. What, are you jealous? We break up and you become some fucking—"

"Okay, that's it," Julia says, and her voice is so loud I think half the cafeteria is looking at us. "Trent, I don't know who pissed in your cornflakes today, but you need to leave. *Now.*"

Chris looks back and forth between the two of them, but we know what's going to happen. He'll side with Julia no matter what.

"Fine," Trent says, and pushing back from our table with a

loud scrape of his chair, he storms off.

And then it's just me and Julia and Chris.

"Thanks," I say, and they both smile at me.

Julia opens her mouth like she's going to say something, but a second before she does, my phone rings.

I look down. 336 area code. Has to be Aldersgate.

"Hello?" I say, picking up.

Julia squeezes my hand under the table.

"Hi, Corinne. Is this a bad time? It's Coach Alma from Aldersgate College."

"H-hi," I say. "No, it's okay."

"Perfect. I'm calling because we have an offer for you."

"Ma'am?"

"We want to know if you want to run for us," she says. "We'd be offering a substantial scholarship."

Why me?

I don't realize I've asked it until Coach Alma laughs uncomfortably. "Well, we think you'd be a great asset to our college."

"But I—I stumbled. I didn't think I did that well."

"We can excuse some nerves. And I've been talking to your coach, and she tells me you've been having a great season . . ."

She continues on, droning, but all I can hear in my head is *scholarship scholarship come out come out keep running—*

"Corinne?"

"Yeah, I'm here."

"So how does next Monday sound?"

"Ma'am?"

"For getting your decision back to us," she says.

"Monday sounds good," I say, and we exchange goodbyes and hang up.

I stare down at my phone like it's betrayed me.

"Who was that?" Julia asks.

"Aldersgate wants me to make a decision," I say, stuffing my phone back in my pocket.

But she doesn't ask anything else, and for that, I'm grateful.

My head is blurry at practice. The rest of the day all I can think about is Trent calling me a bitch and Aldersgate's offer and *why me* and *come out* and Elissa and Maggie—

We're running laps around the track while Coach times us, and my thoughts are so full I don't notice when I've caught up to Haley and we end up tangled, tripping, and she rights herself, but I lose my balance and fall.

My knee scrapes on the ground, and I get up and limp around the rest of the track, swear under my breath, put a Band-Aid on when I get to the locker room.

I am losing it.

Everyone glances around and looks at me, whispers behind hands as they're changing that only die down when Coach comes in.

She talks to us about State, about winning, about expectations, but everyone looks at me and I don't hear a word.

FORTY-SIX DAYS G O N E.

It's the day before State Championships. Julia texts me to come hang out, stretch, practice one more time.

But then Elissa texts me asking if I'll meet her at the park Maggie and I used to go to.

Can't, Julie. Gotta talk to Elissa, I text, and then mute my notifications from her so I don't have to see how she'll respond.

I shouldn't be going to talk to Elissa today. I should be training with Julia.

I should be doing a lot of things, making a lot more decisions than I am.

How am I supposed to decide whether or not to leave, to go to college? I know what I'm supposed to want, and it's to get as far away from here as possible.

But there's my mom. If I go to college, if I don't visit her anymore, what's going to happen to her? Who she was before is buried under a facade of acrylic nails and old booze, and I know I can't bring her back, but if I am the perfect daughter, maybe I can.

I get out of bed and shimmy into a pair of skinny jeans and a sweatshirt, Bysshe purring at the end of my bed.

Mom isn't my problem. I have bigger things to worry about.

I pull my hair back and scratch Bysshe behind his ears before heading out to my car to go meet Elissa. Dad's sitting downstairs on the couch.

"Where are you headed?" he asks.

"Going out to meet Julia before State," I lie, and head out before I have to tell him anything else.

Elissa's standing by the swings when I pull up, hands in the pockets of her army jacket. She got a haircut; the sides of her head are freshly shaved and her curls piled on top. I can see the glowing tip of her cigarette from my car.

"Hey," she says as I walk up, and she leans in to kiss me. I stiffen, but I let her—no one's around to see us, right?

"Hey," I say. "What . . . what did you want to talk about?"

We sit down on the swings, and they creak under our weight. Elissa throws her cigarette down and stomps on it before pushing back and swinging.

"Elissa . . ."

"Hang on," she says, and begins to swing higher.

Did Maggie bring her here? Is that how she knows about this place?

There is so much I don't know about Elissa, about her relationship with Maggie. I look at the girl swinging next to me and I realize I don't know her, not really.

Maggie knew her. Maggie knew all these things about her and about me, things I want to know, things I would tell her if she asked.

But I am not Maggie.

She finally comes back down, cheeks flushed. "Haven't done that in ages," she says, before touching my knee with her own. "I know we haven't talked about us, much, but I wanted to ask—if you maybe wanted to date?"

"I . . ."

"We don't have to, this can just stay casual or whatever, but if—if we date then you need to know I'm not going back in the closet for you."

come out come out come out—

It's not her voice, though. It's Maggie's.

If we're going to keep dating, you need to come out.

No.

You didn't deserve her.

I can't think about that. I can't. Not now.

She pushes off the swing, stands, hands jammed in her pockets.

"Elissa—"

"You know what? Never mind. I'm not doing this. You aren't ready." She shakes her head, then stops. Stares at me. "Maggie wanted you to be out, didn't she?"

My mouth is dry.

"Yes."

"And you didn't."

"No," I say. "No. You asked why we weren't out and—and—"

And it was because of me.

If we're going to keep dating, I need you to come out. If you still want to be together.

"Corinne?"

If you still want to be together.

"I can't do this," I say. "I'm sorry, Elissa, but I can't—"

I run away from her.

TWO DAYS BEFORE.

She's asleep next to me, the warmth of her back pressing into my side, and I know.

I have to break up with her.

She wants us to be out, and it's hurting her that we're not, and I want to be so badly but I am so, so terrified. And she doesn't deserve that, and I don't deserve her.

I have to break up with her.

FORTY-SEVEN DAYS G O N E.

I can't sleep. It's like the night I stayed with her before she died, my thoughts racing, my head too full. I can't sleep, so I don't. I turn on my phone and lie there and listen to every single voice mail from Maggie.

"*You must . . . heh, you must be asleep or something. Were we going to the movies later? Dylan wants to know.*"

"*I can't stop thinking about you.*"

"*Was . . . was that okay? That we kissed? Because if not, I'm sorry. We don't have to do this. I—shit, I'll call you later okay?*"

"*Hey, babe, just got out of* Hairspray *rehearsal. Can't wait for you to come see the show. Everyone's worked so hard—*"

"*Okay, maybe it'll work this time. I just wanted to leave you a message 'cause I feel like it—*"

Her laugh. Her voice in my ear, and before I can stop myself, I log into Instagram, scroll down to that photo of us.

No one has written any new comments in weeks. It's a

strange memorial, like graffiti and just as permanent.

I write. I write a thousand messages until my name is the only thing I see. I write I miss you, over and over and over and over.

And then—

I delete every single comment. Every voice mail except the one where she's laughing. Every text from Elissa.

And I hide

my

stupid

treacherous

traitorous

heart.

I don't sleep the rest of the night. I toss and turn, and when my alarm goes off it's all I can do to get up and get dressed for Championships.

Dad and I eat breakfast together, quietly, not talking about the upcoming race. I know he thinks it's because of nerves, but the truth is I just don't know what to say.

"Sleep okay?" he asks.

"Fine," I say, and that's the most we say to each other until it's almost time to leave.

It's here.

State Championships.

I am setting foot on a course Maggie has never run, a course Dylan has never seen his sister at. Where she always, always wanted to be.

I never expected to be here without her.

But I can't think that. Push it down, run it out. Think about winning, think about scholarships, think about getting out of here and finally being free, finally being able to be myself.

Then why am I so terrified? Why do I feel like I'm making the biggest mistake of my life?

"Hey," Julia says, nudging me with her shoulder. "You okay?"

"Fine."

"I can't believe we're here!" Haley says excitedly. She's even grinning at me. "Can you believe it? We made it to State!"

I nod. Swallow.

They made it.

I made it. I'm here.

Somewhere in the crowd is my dad. Somewhere in the crowd is Elissa, if she bothered to come after yesterday.

Somewhere in the crowd is Maggie, watching, jealous that she could never get here.

I don't want to see her.

I tighten my ponytail, tie her scrunchie around it for luck.

This is it.

If I run hard enough today, then I will stop chasing Maggie, she will stop showing up at the corners of my vision, she will be gone and I will be brave enough, finally, finally brave enough, to talk about who she was to me.

We stretch at the starting line. There's anticipation and humming in the air, hundreds of teen-girl running dreams, gold-medal shiny dreams filling the air so much they're almost palpable.

If Julia does well, she can finally get out of here, she can go to a fancy school and have a long-distance relationship with Chris and it will be fine.

If Haley does well, she'll finally prove to herself that she is not her older sister the track star, that she's someone to be admired in her own right.

If I win . . .

If I . . .

The gun goes off.

And we run.

And I run.

My feet pound the dirt and I push myself hard, so hard, so I can be fast because if I run fast enough the world will spin back into place, Maggie will be alive and I will know what I want.

What I want.

Is it this?

Do I want this?

I wanted Maggie.

I'm sorry I never told her how much. I'm sorry I couldn't be the girl she saw me as.

I loved her, I loved her, I loved her. I don't know who I am without her. She wanted me to be all these big, grand things; she had these dreams for us and—

That's not me. I am not out and proud; I am scared out of my mind. Maggie *wanted*, so I didn't have to.

I loved her but she saw all the good parts of me, and I don't think they're here without her. She saw a girl who was ambitious and dreamed, and now I'm beginning to realize that my dreams involved her. Maggie had dreams and plans and goals and all I wanted to do was to follow her to the ends of the earth.

But I don't think that's what I want anymore.

I don't think I want this.

I don't think I want to win.

I don't want to run anymore. From Elissa. From Maggie.

At all.

I don't want to run.

I am tired of running.

Everyone is cheering and Julia is passing me and Haley is passing me and I can't see Maggie's ponytail in front of me anymore, I could never see it because *it wasn't there*, because she's dead and she isn't coming back and she made me a better person but I need to accept that what she wanted isn't what I want.

I don't want this.

So I.

Slow.

Down.

Everyone else passes me.

Everyone else runs toward their dreams.

Everyone else runs and runs and passes me

until I am dead

last.

Until I am jogging across that finish line and I stop, and I
know.

I am done running.

I cross the finish line and I keep going, past the judges and
the spectators and Julia and Haley and Coach and my dad's disappointment. Past all of it. I run farther into the park, through
the trees, don't care about the branches hitting my arms or my
face. I run like my heart is actually in it, like I should have run
at State.

"Corinne!"

It's a male voice. Not my dad. I skid to a halt, out of breath,
and there's Dylan, pushing through the brambles and the trees.

"What are you doing here?" I ask, and I don't know if I'm
asking about him being here at State or here in these woods
with me, or here at all even though his sister isn't.

"I saw you—come in last. And keep running. I think your
team's looking for you."

"I don't want to see them," I say.

"I figured."

"So why are you here?" I ask.

He frowns. "Because you are."

"And?"

"And you're the last thing I have of my sister and her running and I—I thought—" He shakes his head. "It doesn't matter what I thought."

I nod. I'm standing there and there are branches tangling around my legs and scratching my calves and my dead girlfriend's brother is standing in front of me reminding me of all the ways I am lost without her.

"Come with me," Dylan says.

I shake my head. "I can't."

"Can't what?"

"Can't—can't do this anymore! I can't be out, but I can't hide; I can't pretend that every time I run I'm not envisioning her beside me; I can't—" A sob chokes my voice. "I can't believe she isn't here."

I can't believe I'm doing this without her.

The next time he looks at me, his eyes are shining.

"Come on," he says, more insistently. "I have somewhere I want to show you."

And I don't know why, maybe it's because today has already been awful enough and I have nothing left to lose, but I follow him to his car. He's parked far enough away that we don't run into my teammates or my dad or anyone from Leesboro.

I buckle my seat belt and pull my knees up to my chest and then as he shuts the door I'm crying for real; tears are dripping down my face and when I pull my hands away from my eyes they're smudged with black, and I'm a mess. God. Such a fucking mess.

Dylan flicks his headlights on and wordlessly hands me a few crumpled-up napkins from his glove box. He turns the radio on low to some country station I like, a station Maggie would never have let him play.

His car doesn't smell like her. I thought it would, but it doesn't, and I guess I'm grateful for that.

We drive in silence for a minute before he sighs, rakes his hands through his hair.

"Maggie told me," he says.

"Told you what?" I ask, but something in me tells me I already know the answer.

"The morning after you left. She told me about her ultimatum. About you coming out." He shakes his head. "What were you going to do?"

I don't answer him, and that's answer enough.

"You were going to break up with her," he says.

"Dylan . . ."

His voice goes quiet. "My sister died without anyone

knowing about the one person she cared about most in this world and it's all your damn fault."

I don't say anything. Can't say anything. Because he's right.

"You're a fucking coward, Corinne Parker."

My fingers tighten on the door handle and memory slams into me, everything I've been trying to forget since Maggie died, all of it rushing back in a tidal wave of all my awful mistakes.

EIGHT MONTHS BEFORE.

"I . . . I like you, too," I say. "And I don't—I don't know what I am and I'm trying to figure that out but Maggie, I *really* like you, and—"

She kisses me again. Leans over across the swing and presses her lips to mine, her mouth soft and cold.

"Do you . . . do you want to maybe try this? Us? Dating?" she asks, and I kiss her back, hoping she knows what my answer is.

"Yeah," I say. "I do." I grin, and it fills my whole face, and I kiss her again. She stands, looking around at the rest of the park.

"Are you going to tell your parents?" she asks.

I blink. "What?"

"About—about us? Are you going to come out?"

"Um. I haven't thought about it," I say, and I haven't, because I've shoved it to the back of my mind where it doesn't Mean

Anything, because I barely even know what it means myself, liking her, wanting to kiss her.

She nods. "Okay. I mean—I told my brother. About you—about how much I like you."

"You told your brother?"

"I tell him everything," she says, like it's simple, like it's just that fucking simple to tell your brother who's a religious studies major that you're into girls. Or *a* girl.

"I . . ."

She turns and looks at me, a frown creasing the spot between her eyebrows. "I don't need your permission to tell my brother about us."

"I know that," I say, but my heart hammers away in my chest all the same.

She sighs, comes back over to the swing, and takes my hand. "I'm not asking you to come out right now," she says. "But . . . but down the road . . . at least think about it, okay?"

"Okay," I say, and swallow. "Yeah. Okay. I will."

She smiles, and leans in and kisses me again.

This time when her lips meet mine, all I taste is fear.

FIVE MONTHS BEFORE.

Her brother disappears up the stairs. Maggie's brother.

"He's going to tell." My voice rises in panic.

"He's not going to tell," Maggie soothes, her hands in mine. "Calm down."

"Your parents can't find out." My voice, high and shrill the way I hate when I'm angry or upset or scared like now.

"They won't find out. I promise."

I put my head on her shoulder, but the contact is too much, too much of a reminder so I stand, begin pacing her basement back and forth.

"Maggie, they can't find out," I say, and I look at her.

"I know," she says. "No one can find out."

But there's resignation in her voice.

ONE MONTH BEFORE.

"Why can't you just be with me?" she yells, her cheeks splotchy and red and her eyes shining.

"I want to!"

"No, you don't," she spits. "You're too scared of what everyone else will think."

SEVEN MONTHS BEFORE.

It's growing dark as we walk to the restaurant, the days still short. Maggie's in a cute blue dress and tights, dark gray coat and scarf around her neck. Her cheeks are flushed pink, and when she smiles at me, it's like I can't see anyone else.

She reaches for my hand as we cross the street, intertwines her gloved fingers with mine.

But everyone is staring; I know it. They're all staring at our fingers intertwined and they know they know they know—

I pull my hand away from hers. I want to tell her I'm sorry, I'm scared, and it's Valentine's Day and I just want to be able to enjoy this time with my girlfriend, I'm sorry—

But it doesn't make a difference. She's heard me say it before.

I wish I were braver. I wish I could hold her hand without wanting to pull away, without caring what everyone thinks, without worrying if it's safe.

I wish I could be braver for her.

But I'm not. I'm a coward.

And we both know it.

SIX MONTHS BEFORE.

"I just don't get what you're so damn afraid of!"

SEVEN MONTHS BEFORE.

"I don't want to do this now," I hear myself saying.

"You never want to! You never want to do this, Corinne. You don't want to come to prom with me, you wouldn't hold my hand when we went out for Valentine's Day, and you don't even want to come to the show when you know how hard I've worked on it!" She sniffs. Wipes her eyes.

"Are you ashamed to be with me?"

ONE WEEK BEFORE.

We're at that park again, the one she loves. It's so hot my thighs stick to the back of the chair when I stand.

She's quiet, quieter than normal.

"You okay?"

She shakes her head. "I've been thinking about us."

"Oh."

"Corinne . . . I want to be out with you. I really do. And if—if that's too hard for you, then you need to tell me."

"I . . ."

"I need you to decide," she says, her voice firmer. "If you still want to be with me, you need to come out. We've been together eight months, and I—I don't want to pressure you, but I'm really, really tired of hiding this."

I take her hand. "I know," I say. "I know."

FORTY-SEVEN DAYS G O N E.

I'm crying in Dylan's car as I'm telling him this, as I'm remembering everything we fought about, every time I wouldn't hold her hand, every time I pulled away from her, every fight and scream and word in excruciating detail and over and over again—

Are you ashamed to be with me?

It was never her I was ashamed of, never her I was ashamed to be with. It was me. My fear. My own shame, my terror at what everyone would think of me if we were out together.

I don't know what I expect from Dylan—if I expect anything. Pity. Rage. Something. Anything but this awful, unbearable silence full of judgment.

I reach for my phone, something to give my hands to do. But it's dead, so I reach for the charger plugged into Dylan's car.

"Can I?" I ask, and he looks down and nods, his hands still on the steering wheel.

"You should text your dad," Dylan says. "Or your coach. Just so they don't worry."

"Where are we going?" I ask sourly as he pulls onto a back road.

"You'll see," he says, and I close my eyes as Dylan drives me toward some great unknown and away from my grief.

Dylan drives up to this remote area, puts his car in park, and for a second I'm worried something's going to happen, even though it's Dylan, because that's what we do, we girls—a boy drives you somewhere alone and it doesn't matter how much you trust or know him because you can never tell.

"Where are we?" I ask, but he doesn't answer, just gets out of the car and slams the door, and I follow. It's cold out here in my shorts, and I tug at the edges of them, but it doesn't do any good.

Dylan walks out of the gravel parking lot and I follow him, and suddenly we're standing at the edge of this bridge I've never been to, overlooking some river rushing below us. Dylan sits down, his long, pale legs dangling over the side. He doesn't motion for me to sit with him, and for a minute I'm not even sure if I want to. But after a minute of awkwardly shifting back and forth, I sit, and he speaks like he's just been sitting there waiting for me to do that the whole time.

"My sister loved this place," he says quietly, swinging his legs back and forth. I'm not even sure he's aware he's doing it. "We used to come here a lot before I left for college and talk, which I know everyone thought was weird because brothers and sisters are supposed to fight all the time. And yeah, we did, but she knew how to get me to open up and talk it out, too. Once I started driving, I'd bring her here, and it's the one thing I really missed when I went to Duke.

"You know, one night I was at school and I get a text at two in the morning and it's Mags, and it just says 'Bridge?' And she never wanted to meet anymore unless it was important, so I drove all the way out here from Durham at two in the morning, and when I got here, she was standing, and . . . she looked so goddamn happy. And she doesn't even wait for me to walk up before the words are out of her mouth and she's telling me about this girl she'd met and how she was so excited about her and how wonderful she was."

He looks down at his hands. Clears his throat. "Obviously she was talking about you." He laughs, and it's low and angry. "I don't know what she saw in you," he says, and it's that that hurts the most, because I don't know what she saw in me, either.

"She wasn't some martyr," I say quietly. "You should know that."

"I do. I grew up with her."

"I loved her," I say. "I know you don't think I did. But I did. And she wasn't perfect and she . . . she put up with a lot from me, but she loved me too."

302

"Corinne—"

"I'm scared of a lot, you know. She knew that." I blow out through my bangs. "You know what?" I ask Dylan. "On Valentine's Day we went out to this nice restaurant downtown Raleigh—didn't tell anybody. And it was great, but after we walked to this coffee shop and I wouldn't let her hold my hand and she got so *mad* at me. She said we were downtown; nothing was going to happen to us. And we fought about it and I found out later she was pissed because some girl in her math class had asked her what she was doing for Valentine's Day and she'd had to lie. And whenever I think about her, I think how I wouldn't hold her hand, and now . . .

"I'm scared, Dylan," I say, and admitting it out loud just sets me crying again. "I'm scared of what everyone else will think of me. I'm scared of it being a big deal and I'm scared if everyone knows then all I'll be when they see me is *that girl*."

"It wasn't like that for Elissa. Or Maggie."

"Have you seen Elissa? She couldn't be in the closet if she tried."

"Corinne."

"No, you're right, that was really bitchy." I shake my head. "I just . . . worry about what everyone else thinks too much to be out."

"You know no one's asking you to dye your hair rainbow and kiss a bunch of girls, right? And it's not as bad as it used to be—"

"Yeah, tell me how bad coming out is, straight white boy," I say.

"You really are a bitch."

"And here I thought we were having a moment," I say. I swing my legs harder. "I know it's not as bad as it used to be. And it won't be as bad for me as some people. But that doesn't mean I'm not terrified; it doesn't mean that Maggie being gone doesn't *hurt*." I suck in a breath. "She would've won today. I know she would have. She would've won and gone on to Villanova and she would've been this big star if I wasn't—if I wasn't just holding her back—"

My voice grows thick again. Dylan waits for a moment, then places his hand on mine.

"She wasn't going to leave you," he says softly. "She—she wanted to defer Villanova, do a year at Aldersgate with you and maybe transfer."

I can't hear this.

"No, she—she wouldn't have done that."

"She would have. She was going to call the Villanova coach and turn them down. Accept Aldersgate's offer instead."

"I'm glad she didn't," I say. "And maybe I wouldn't have said that when she was alive, but Dylan . . . I can't believe she'd put her dream on hold like that."

"You don't get it," he says.

"I dated her. I loved her. What the fuck don't I get?"

"She didn't think you were holding her back, Corinne. Not from that. She—she knew she was good enough. She just wanted to be with you." He sighs. "She loved you more than she loved running."

And maybe I love running away more than I loved her.

The thought stuns me, causes my fists to clench. I stand up. "Can you drive me so I can pick up my car?"

He nods, but he stays sitting.

"Please, Dylan," I say when he doesn't move. "Please just let me go home and forget, okay?"

He sighs, shoves his hands in his pockets. "I'm sorry," he finally says. "I know you loved her. And it's hard, and I don't know anything about it, but—it hurt watching her worry about you. It really hurt."

"It hurt me too," I say, and he nods as we get in the car.

"You know why I brought you here? Why I even came to this race?"

"I don't want to hear it. Just take me home."

But he doesn't start the car. I look over at him, and his eyes are as bright as mine.

"She wanted to show this place to you," he says quietly. "She told me. And I—I wanted to, because she never got that chance. She didn't get the chance to be at State, either, and I thought—watching you run, I thought . . . that it's the closest I'll get to seeing her again."

He wipes at his eyes with his hand and starts the car.

I twist around in my seat as he does, watching that clearing, that bridge, just get smaller and smaller, until it's gone.

Until it disappears entirely.

TWO DAYS BEFORE.

I don't know if I want to do this anymore.

Hide.

I can tell she doesn't; she pulls away when I try to kiss her.

I want to apologize to her. For everything, for hiding, for making her hide part of herself.

We have another sleepover. Dylan looks at us when I enter the house, but no one says anything. We watch some comedy with her parents, and afterward we sleep in her bed and kiss for hours.

If we come out this is over.

And I can't be brave enough for her.

I love her. This is going to hurt her, hurt me, but I've hurt her enough the past few months.

I love her so, so much, and that's why I have to let her go.

FORTY-SEVEN DAYS G O N E.

I pull up to my mom's around three. My phone is charged, and when I turn it on the messages start pouring in.

From Julia:

Where are you?

why'd you stop?

everyone's looking for you

call me

shit corinne i'm worried

your dad said you left

call me later okay?

There are two messages from my dad, right after I told him I was going to Mom's.

We need to talk

Call me Monday after school before you come home.

The last message is from Elissa, and it's that one that sets my heart pounding.

I'm sorry.

I want to ask her what for. Making me feel like I have to come out of the closet? Having feelings for me?

I respond to my dad, and Julia, and delete Elissa's message from my phone.

Mom's cooking when I come in, and the house smells like pasta sauce. She turns around when the dogs start yapping.

"Corey?" she says. "I wasn't expecting you."

"Yeah, I know."

"Have you been running?"

I stare at her. "State Championships were today."

She keeps stirring.

"Mom?"

Nothing. I kick at the kitchen chair.

"What?"

"I said Championships were today. State Championships."

I don't know why I suddenly care that she wasn't there. Maybe because she hasn't been when I wanted her to be, maybe because today, for months, since Maggie died, since we moved, I've just needed her there.

"Why didn't you come?" I ask, and my voice sounds hollow.

She stops stirring.

"Your dad asked me not to," she says finally.

"What?"

I can't believe I'm hearing this, after everything today.

"He asked me not to come."

"To what? To State or to all my meets? Because you haven't been to a single one since I started running."

"That's not true, Corinne," she says. "I went to the first one."

"Well, I didn't see you."

"That's because you don't remember," she says.

We're standing, staring at each other, hands on hips, and I'm reminded of all the ways I'm like her.

"Why did Dad ask you not to come?" I say.

Her lips tighten. I think we both know the answer. "He thought you would lose focus if I was there," she finally says.

"Or did he think you'd embarrass us?"

I can't believe I said it. One of the dogs yaps at my feet. My mother's eyes narrow. "That was uncalled for," she says. "I wanted to be there, Corinne."

"But you didn't even try, did you?" I snap, and suddenly it's all pouring out. "I needed you at my races, here—I just need you to be present without being drunk all the time, but that seems like too much to ask, because you don't even notice me anymore. I can't even talk to you and I—"

I'm crying. I'm crying for Maggie and who I was before and Elissa and my mother. And when I finally wipe my eyes, she's crying, too.

"I stopped running," I say. "But you don't even care, do you? You weren't even there. I came in last today and I don't want to run anymore and I—I could have used you, Mom, because the only reason I even ran in the first place is—" I choke up. "Is because of this girl."

ONE YEAR BEFORE.

I can't stop thinking about her.

That girl. Maggie.

Why can't I stop thinking about her? About how she looked at me, about how touching her hand felt, about . . .

about kissing her why am I thinking about kissing her? About what it would be like?

Am I . . .

Am I gay?

Bi?

Oh my God. Am I bi?

I liked Trent, I really did, but I . . . I think I like Maggie, too. In the same way.

I was going to quit running. This year. I was going to tell Julia I quit, that I didn't want to do it anymore, but if I keep running I can see her, if I keep running I can get out of here, get a scholarship and get far away, if I . . .

I think about what it would be like to kiss her.

I think I want to.

I want to kiss her. I will keep running if it means I get to run after her.

FORTY-SEVEN DAYS G O N E.

I tell her. In seconds and minutes and hours. I tell her about Maggie, about us, about Trent, about Julia and Chris and Elissa and Dylan and the weight of everyone else's grief and expectations. I tell her about Aldersgate, about meeting Sneha and Olivia. I tell her about kissing girls and kissing boys and how scared I am of what everyone else will think.

I'm done crying by the time I finish talking. I don't know if I have any more tears left.

"So yeah," I say. "I just . . . I needed you there for this, Mom."

We're sitting at the kitchen table. I have a glass in front of me. So does she. It's filled with water.

When I finally look up at her, her eyes are brimming again. She pulls me in for a hug.

"I'm sorry," she says into my hair. Her voice is raw, nails around the edges. "I'm sorry I wasn't there for you. I've been a shitty mom."

"No, you haven't," I say. My heart still thuds in my chest. "And that's not the only reason I didn't tell you. I thought you wouldn't take it seriously. Take me seriously."

She nods. "That's fair, I guess."

"So . . . what do you think?" I ask, and I'm holding my breath, waiting for a response, a confirmation, something any- thing so I know what to do.

"About the fact you're bi? I don't mind, Corey," she says, and she turns and smiles at me and I know she's telling the truth. "I love you no matter what. Even if I don't show it that well."

"Mom . . ."

"I'm sorry you felt like you had to lie about it," she continues. "I'm sorry you didn't tell us about Maggie. God, what that girl's family must be going through . . ." She stops and sighs.

"I can't imagine losing you without knowing about those parts of you, Corinne—all of them," she says, and she's crying and then she's hugging me, her long nails scratching my back through my shirt and I thought I didn't have more tears left but I guess I do, because I'm crying into her shirt, because I don't want her to lose me, either.

I don't want to be lost.

FORTY-NINE DAYS G O N E.

No one speaks to me at school Monday except Julia. The girls on the cross-country team all glare at me through class, through lunch, and I eat alone in the science room.

We still placed third, because it only takes the first five girls for the score to count. Julia and Haley both won individual medals, and the girls crowd around them and talk about how proud they are.

Did you hear Corinne just gave up? Did you hear she came in last?

It threads through their gossip so carelessly, in between talk of who applied to what college and who's leaving town for Christmas.

Coach sits us down at practice, even though the season's over, just so we can debrief. I don't hear a word she says, and as the locker room empties and everyone leaves, I barely register someone sitting down next to me.

"Why'd you do it?"

Julia.

"I don't know."

"Yes, you do." She nudges my leg with her own. "I know everyone thought this was what you wanted, but—be honest with me, Corinne."

How do I tell her that I don't think I ever wanted to run in the first place? That no, I didn't want this? This is what Maggie wanted for me, what everyone else wanted for me.

I don't want to run. I'm tired of running, tired of chasing the ghost of a girl who can't love me anymore. Tired of chasing someone else's dreams for me.

"I don't know," I say, fidgeting. "I . . . if I'm being honest, Julia, I ran because of her. I think I stopped running for me, you know? Like . . . I don't want to run anymore. From anything."

She nods. "State was a really inconvenient time for you to figure that out, Corinne. I—how could you be so selfish?"

Selfish.

God. I am selfish.

"I'm sorry," I say quietly. "I'm really, really sorry."

She nods. "I'm still pissed at you, you know."

"I know. Did you win anything? I didn't stick around."

"I got fourth," Julia says.

"Damn."

"Yeah."

"Your parents proud?"

"I think so."

"Chris proud?"

She nods. "He is."

There's something she isn't telling me.

"Did you tell him?" I ask.

She nods again. "I did."

"And?"

"And he's supportive. It's going to take some time for us both to figure out, especially since we'll probably go to different colleges and we have to talk about whether or not we want to do the long-distance thing, but it's okay. He understands. I think he was just relieved to know what was going on with me," she says.

"That's . . . that's great."

"Yeah," she says. "Hey. Speaking of college, did you ever call Aldersgate back?" There's a slight hint of panic in her voice, panic that should be in mine.

But what if I don't want to leave?

I think back to all the stories my dad told me, that I've seen from everyone else, the girls who sell Avon, Dad's brother who lives an hour away and farms, and I want to know—why are these bad things?

What if I don't know what I want right now? What if I don't have big dreams for myself, big dreams for what I want, at least not right now? What if all I want right now is to graduate high school and stay at home and figure it out from there? Why is that any less valid than Julia's dreams of Division I colleges, of Chris's dreams of NFL football, of Trent and Haley's dreams of leaving here?

Why do I have to want what everyone else wants me to?

"I turned them down," I say. And I did. Sent an email last night because I was too scared to call.

She nods. "That's what you want, then, yeah?"

What I want?

"Yeah," I say, and I reach over and squeeze her hand. "I think it is."

We sit like that for a minute, fingers intertwined.

"Oh," I say. "I told my mom. About being bi."

"How'd she take it?" Julia asks.

"She listened, so that's a start."

"You tell her about Elissa?"

I fidget. "Yeah. But it doesn't matter. We . . . I don't know what we are anymore."

"What happened?"

I tell her what Elissa and Dylan told me. About Maggie staying in the closet for me. About how she would have stayed home for me. About all the ways I failed her as a girlfriend.

Julia holds up a hand, stops me. "Corinne, you didn't fail her. That's bullshit. You weren't ready. That's okay. And look, I didn't know Maggie, but she should've been honest with you.

So should Elissa. You deserve someone who's going to be honest with you," she says.

"I know. And I . . . I don't even know how I feel about Elissa. If I like her."

"Maybe you should talk to her? I mean it sounds like you left things kinda rough, so . . . you know."

I should, I know.

"And Corey? Maybe you should tell your dad, too. He's kinda been in the dark, hasn't he?"

"Yeah, maybe," I say.

The locker room door creaks open and Haley rushes in, pale cheeks flushed. "Sorry. Forgot my sweatpants."

She stops, stares at us. "What're y'all talking about?"

"My possible girlfriend," I say, and it only takes her a moment before she grins at me.

This is my coming out. One person at a time. No big statement, no grand gesture. Only people I want to tell.

Why should I come out the way everyone else wants me to?

I call Dad before I drive home, but the only response I get is voice mail, even though he told me to call him.

He isn't home when I pull up. I have no idea where he is. Bysshe is meowing insistently by his food bowl, so I give him a treat, stroke his fur.

I came out to Haley today. And I wasn't scared; I didn't die. It went okay. The world didn't implode.

I can do this.

I wait an hour and Dad still doesn't show up. I think about what Julia said, how I should talk to Elissa about us, about what we are.

No time like the present, right?

I call her.

"Hey," I say. "Can you come over? We need to talk."

I don't wait for her to respond when I hang up. It's on her now, to show up or not.

God, I hope she does.

Elissa pulls up about fifteen minutes later. My hands fidget on my thighs; I haven't been still since I called her. Bysshe jumps off my lap and meows at the window when her truck pulls up.

And then the doorbell's ringing and she's there and I don't know what to do.

We need to talk. We need to sit down and talk about us and everything *and and and—*

But I open the door and then she's standing there and she's in my house and she is gorgeous and I don't know what to think. There are so many things I don't know about her, about Maggie, about myself.

"Hi," she says.

"Hi," I say, and I step back to let her in.

She looks tired. As tired as I feel, maybe.

"I heard about State," she says. She's standing awkwardly in my living room, and Bysshe is eyeing her suspiciously and it's all I can think that she's seeing part of my life Maggie never did, because Maggie never came over, because we—

"Dylan tell you?"

"Yeah," she says. "Can I . . . can I sit?"

"Yeah," I say, and follow suit. We sit on opposite ends of the couch, not looking at each other. Elissa absently strokes Bysshe's fur. He purrs.

"What's his name?"

"Bysshe."

"Like Percy Shelley?"

I blink. She looks over at me, finally. Shrugs. "I had a huge crush on Mary Shelley in high school and did a shit ton of research about her. Though Percy was a bit of an ass."

"I wouldn't know. My dad named him," I say. "Though yeah, the cat can be an asshole."

She laughs at that.

"What'd your text mean?" I ask.

She stops laughing, and when she looks at me, I want to flinch away from the intensity of her gaze.

"I'm just . . . sorry. For this," she says, hands moving between us. "For us. For giving you an ultimatum on coming out. I shouldn't—I shouldn't have done that."

"No. You shouldn't," I say, my voice cold, and she nods. "Elissa, I like you. I really—I really do, and not just because of

Maggie, or—or all of that. But I . . . I don't know if I'm ready for another relationship."

She nods. "Yeah. That's . . . that's okay. I probably need some time, too," she says. "So . . . do you wanna try just being friends for a bit? Maybe? We don't have to if you don't want—and I get it if it's easier to have me out of your life completely, you know?"

I do.

But I need a friend, I need someone who knows what Maggie was like, who I can talk about her with. Who I don't have to hide from.

"Yeah," I say. "Friends—that'd be nice."

She nods. "Yeah. Good. I'm . . . I'm gonna go, okay? But call me, or text me, or whatever—anytime you want to talk."

"Okay."

She stands, heads toward the door, and then turns and looks back at me. "Corinne?"

"Yeah?"

"I really am sorry," she says.

"I am too," I say, and she leaves and the door quietly shuts.

But I feel a little less empty as she goes.

Dad's car pulls up only a few minutes later, and he enters the front door with a bag of groceries.

"Thought I'd make dinner tonight," he says, and heads to the kitchen.

That's it. No mention of State, or being out, or how I failed, or staying with my mother, or—

"Dad?"

"Chicken breast okay?" he asks.

"That's fine, but Dad—"

He ignores me. Puts the chicken in a pan, puts the pan in the oven. Shuts it and goes to the sink to wash his hands.

"Dad, can we talk?"

He turns the water off, stands there with his hands still dripping. My hands are on my hips.

This isn't me. I don't do confrontation. Neither did my mother, neither does my dad, and maybe that's why they got divorced—because no one wants to talk about the ugly parts of this family.

"What, Corinne?" he says. His glasses are falling down his nose.

"I . . . I'm not going to college," I blurt out.

Silence. One. Two. Three minutes. Bysshe meows. The sink drips, and my dad and I stand and stare at each other with the echoes of my words in the air.

"Does this have anything to do with the stunt you pulled at State?" he asks.

"Maybe?" I sigh. "I just . . . I don't want to run anymore."

No running means no scholarship means no college. You know that, don't you?

I've always known that.

But what if I'm okay with that?

"I just don't understand," Dad says. "Why you wouldn't want something better for yourself than—than this town, than *here*?"

For the first time, I look at him and I see how he thinks it's his fault that we're trapped here, then I'm crying.

"I don't get why everyone wants me to always strive for something bigger," I say. "Why can't you just be happy with *me*, with where I am now? You're not, Coach isn't, Maggie wasn't—" I take in deep, gasping breaths. "And I'm so tired of trying to be this perfect person that everyone else wants me to be, of wanting what everyone else wants me to!"

My dad dries his hands. Looks me up and down. My chest heaves and I wipe at my eyes with my hands and he passes me the dishtowel.

"Who's Maggie?" he finally says.

And I tell him. About us, about her, about all her goals and plans and dreams for us and everything she wanted me to be— State, Division I, running together on weekends at Villanova and landing on magazine covers by twenty-five. Picture-perfect girls with big dreams and shiny hair.

But that's not me. I don't know if it ever has been, but for her, I was willing to try. Wanted to try, wanted to be that shiny golden girl she saw me as.

When I'm done, Dad's hands are completely dry. My eyes are wet. And then he's hugging me and I'm crying all over again.

"I'm sorry," I say. "Dad, I'm sorry."

He pulls back from me. "Why?"

"Because—because I know you wanted me to get out of here, because I don't—I know how proud you are of me running and Aldersgate and I just—I never want to be a disappointment to you."

"Corinne," he says, and then he pulls me in for another hug. "Listen to me. You are *never* a disappointment to me. I might be disappointed with things you do, but *you* are never a disappointment."

I sniff again. "You sure?"

"Of course," he says. "Of course."

We sit down together, Dad pretending not to look when I sneak Bysshe pieces of chicken.

"So," he says when we're almost done, "you think community college might be a good option?"

"Yeah. It just . . . it'll be easier. And I can stay home and we can save money—you did want me to avoid student loans—and I can still visit Mom, because—yeah, because someone needs to." I look at him. "Speaking of . . . why did you tell her not to come to my meets?"

Something painful crosses my Dad's face, an echo of a fight he must have had with my mother.

"Because," he says after a minute. "I wanted—needed—you to do well. And I thought, running made you happy and I didn't want your mother to sabotage that. And I know, I know that's wrong, Corinne. I shouldn't have."

"Then you should've listened to me, Dad," I say. "About—about it getting bad. With her. Not just banning her from my meets. I could've used her there."

"I know," he says. Then he shifts, clears his throat. "Have you talked with her about . . . all of this?"

"You mean the bisexual stuff?" I can't resist a jab. "Yeah. I have. And she's okay with it."

He nods.

"How're you feeling about it?"

"I'll need time," he says, and a twinge of anxiety forms in my gut. "But that doesn't—that doesn't mean I don't accept you and love you, Corey. It's just, growing up here . . . there's a lot I need to unlearn," he says.

"Yeah," I say. "Me too."

He nods. "So. Got your eye on anyone?"

"*Dad.*"

"I have to ask. It's a dad law."

I shrug. "I don't know. There was this girl, but I . . . I think I might've messed it up, I don't know. She . . . she knew Maggie. So we both just need some time, I guess."

"Fair," he says. He stands and turns back to the sink, stops. "Corinne . . . do you want to talk to someone about this? Someone who isn't me, I mean. I've always . . . I'm always here for you, but some of the stuff you've been dealing with, I'm not really qualified."

I snort. "Qualified?"

"You know what I mean."

I think about it. Therapy. Talking to someone about Maggie and my mom and what they mean to me and everyone else's expectations.

"I think that'd be nice, yeah," I say.

"Good," he says.

"Thanks," I say, and he nods.

"So, community college?"

I shrug. "Maybe. Yeah."

"What do you think you'd major in?"

"I honestly have no idea," I say. "Maybe computer science, like you. Maybe biology. Maybe chemistry. Who says I have to know right now?"

Dad laughs. "You're seventeen. You don't."

"Good," I say.

And I don't have to know. I don't have to have a map, a plan, color-coded schools on a spreadsheet. It's okay that I don't.

It's okay to want things for myself.

TWO MONTHS G O N E.

I'm standing on Dylan's doorstep again, wondering when I shifted to thinking of it as his doorstep instead of Maggie's.

I need to apologize. Say sorry, make right, whatever. He was right. I was selfish. I *am* selfish.

Mrs. Bailey opens the door when I knock. Maggie looked like her. She could have known about us, but she didn't because of me.

"Hello," she says, pleasant enough, her eyes searching my face. "You're Corinne, right? Maggie's friend?"

"I'm actually here to see Dylan," I say, the words coming out in a rush. "Is he home?"

For a second I'm afraid she's going to tell me no, he isn't, that he's gone back to Duke.

"You're in luck: it's his last weekend of winter break," she says, and steps aside to let me enter.

She doesn't tell me where his room is, like she remembered

who I am. I want to tell her I'm sorry her daughter's dead, I'm sorry for her loss.

I can't make myself say it.

I take the stairs up to Dylan's room, knock on his door. He opens it, still in a T-shirt and flannel pants, looks me up and down not unlike his mother did.

"Corinne," he says. "What do you want?"

"I want you to come to her grave with me," I say. "I want . . . I want to give you her stuff back. You were right. I shouldn't keep it; it's not mine. And I . . . I'm sorry. For everything," I say, and I don't know if I'm apologizing to him or his sister.

It takes Dylan a long time to say anything. He runs his hands through his hair, a gesture Maggie did whenever she was trying to think.

"Let me get dressed," he says, finally, and shuts the door on me.

Dylan is quiet on the drive up to Maggie's grave, his knuckles white on the steering wheel. The box of her stuff is in my lap, her scrunchie still around my wrist.

"Are you okay?" I ask.

It's the first time I've asked him that. Since everything. Since finding out she died.

God, why didn't I ask sooner? He lost his sister.

"I don't know," he answers, never taking his eyes off the

road. "I feel like I should be, but I'm not. Or I feel like I am, but I shouldn't be. Grief is . . . grief is weird," he says.

"It is."

"How are you?" he asks as he turns down the street by the cemetery, finally looking at me. "I never really asked you that after States. I'm sorry."

"I'm . . . the same as you, I guess," I say, turning the scrunchie over and over and over on my wrist.

But there's still something unsaid, still something I haven't asked him, something that's been nagging at me since the day she died.

"Dylan?"

We're parked in the lot, the engine still running.

"Why didn't you call me? To tell me she . . . to tell me she died. You called Elissa. Why didn't you call me?"

"Because I was mad at you that no one else would," he says immediately. "Because you didn't want to be out, it automatically fell to me to call you. I know that's selfish—fuck, I know that."

I place my hand over his. "It's okay," I say, and squeeze. A minute later, he grips my hand back. "You're allowed to be selfish. She was your sister."

He nods, stone-faced, and we get out of the car.

I don't cry at the gravesite. Dylan does, though. He cries like no one would let him at the funeral, and I lean into his shoulder as we mourn his sister, my girlfriend, Maggie. We mourn a girl. A messy, hot-tempered, queer, beautiful stubborn girl. Not an angel, not a martyr, not an Instagram picture on someone's account or a ghost for me to chase.

I don't cry until I get home. And then I park my car and cut it off and look at the mark around my wrist where her scrunchie was and think about the box that's now in Dylan's car, and I let myself go.

She's gone. Maggie is gone, and we weren't out because of me, and she isn't coming back no matter how much I want her to. I can't bring her back by running as fast as I can, by kissing Elissa, by wearing her scrunchie.

But I can grieve, I can mourn, and I can remember.

TWO MONTHS G O N E.

The day for everyone to sign their letters of intent comes, and I am not included. We shuffle into the auditorium, parents and students and aunts and uncles and family, and watch as our star athletes line up to declare where they're going.

Everyone looks beautiful. Julia and Chris match, of course, and Haley looks cute in a green dress and Trent looks as good as he did when we dated.

They aren't dating. Haley wants to wait until college, told Trent he needs to learn to think before he opens his mouth. She and I have decided we'll go to winter formal with Julia and Chris and some of the other cross-country girls.

We hold our breath together as Coach Reynolds and Coach Myers announce the school everyone's signing with, as they wait with their pens and letters.

Briefly, I wonder what it would be like to be up there, but then stop. Maggie wanted to be up there, and seeing Julia pick up her pen and declare she's going to Clemson makes the twinge in my chest that much larger.

I am watching my best friend do something Maggie never will. I am measuring everything now in moments she will not get to participate in, things she will not get to do, experiences she won't have, or places she won't go. It's almost Christmas. In one month it will have been a year since I kissed Maggie. It's been three months since she left me, and the ache is still there.

It will be Dylan's first Christmas without his sister, his parents' first without their daughter.

I've promised to check in on him that day. Go with him to the gravesite the day after so he doesn't have to be alone, so I don't have to be alone.

I swallow everything down and cheer for my friends.

Haley signs with Aldersgate, not following in her track-star sister's footsteps. I've already given her Sneha and Olivia's numbers, made her promise to me that I can tag along for Waffle House some night.

Chris and Trent both commit to Appalachian, and we hear they'll go and room together, and maybe Julia will visit on weekends, maybe she won't. I don't feel like I'm supposed to be up there with them anymore. There's no sense of obligation, no fear of not belonging. I sent in my community college application last week. I'm supposed to hear from them soon.

Maybe I'll major in chemistry. Maybe I'll spend my days

in a lab researching, with chemicals and facts and knowledge; maybe I'll stay single or maybe some boy or girl or someone who isn't either of those things on campus will catch my eye, maybe.

I'm not as afraid of what everyone else thinks anymore.

SEVEN MONTHS BEFORE.

We're at the park. Swinging, hands interlocked and sneakers nearly touching the clouds.

When I was a kid, I used to think I could swing high enough to reach over the bar, but I can't do that. Some things are just impossible no matter how hard you try.

Maggie stops swinging, tugging on my hand so she can bring me back down to earth.

She's always leading. I'm always following.

"Corinne?" she says, and her voice is uncertain and soft but she's looking at me.

"Yeah?"

She sighs, wraps our fingers together, and looks at me.

"I love you," she says, and it nearly steals the breath from me.

It's the first time she's said it. We've only been together a few months, tentatively exploring whatever this is we have, stealing kisses in her basement.

But she's here. She's holding my hand.

"I love you, too," I say. And she's smiling and she kisses me and I love her, I love her. She is beautiful and she is a girl and I love her.

And right now, I think I might be okay with that.

NOW.

I have stopped counting how long it's been since she died.

She deserves to be remembered, not measured by the days of my grief or how long it's been since she left. She deserves to be remembered for who she was.

I graduate in two weeks. In two weeks I will do something Maggie never did. I will get out of here. Go to community college. Do science, hang out with Julia on weekends when she's home. Go to AA meetings with my mother, Al-Anon meetings for me. Move back and forth between my parents' houses and always keep a suitcase in my car, just in case.

I am done running from my problems, done chasing the ghost of a girl who cannot love me back. I am here. I am alive, and the girl I was with Maggie isn't here anymore, but I don't have to forget her; I don't have to forget who I was.

Here is what I know:

My name is Corinne Parker. I loved a boy named Trent, a

girl named Maggie. I loved them differently and equally but I loved them and they were real, they mattered.

My parents are divorced. My mother is an alcoholic. She's in recovery and she's trying. My father doesn't see me sometimes, but we talk when it matters. I am not a disappointment.

Here is what I don't know:

Where I'm going to end up in the future. Who I'm going to end up with, if I end up with anyone. What the hell I'm going to do with the rest of my life.

But maybe I don't have to figure it all out right now.

ACKNOWLEDGMENTS

Writing these doesn't feel real. There are so, so many people to thank and so, so many people this book wouldn't be possible without.

First and foremost—Mom and Dad. For Mom: Ich liebe dich, und du bist die beste Mutter der Welt. Dad, since you didn't understand that: I love you so much. I'm so proud to be your daughter. Thank you both for always reading with me, for encouraging me, for taking me to see Laurie Halse Anderson when I was in high school. You're the best parents I could ask for.

To Eric Smith, agent extraordinaire: We did it. Thank you for your perseverance, your emails, your texts, your love and enthusiasm for my sad books. For reassuring my anxious self through every stage of this process. This wouldn't have been possible without you, and I can't wait to see what the future holds.

To Catherine Wallace: Your insights made this book sing,

and it wouldn't have been possible without you. Thank you for championing this book from the beginning and helping to make it really shine.

To the team at HarperTeen: Laura Harshberger, Erin Wallace, Shannon Cox, and Aubrey Churchwood: thank you for believing in my quiet and sad bisexual book. Max Reed and Jessie Gang, thank you for the beautiful cover.

Hannah Dent: Schatz, you are my light and my stars. Thank you for giving me space to write, for making me tea, for being so enthusiastic about this book since you read it. I love you.

To Sneha Gaitonde and Olivia Vigee: I love you both so much I had to include you in fiction. Thank you for all the texts, tumblr chats, wine and wing nights, Food Network binge watching, and so much more. Y'all are the best squad anyone could ask for.

Jean Trevorrow: I'm so glad we met. Thank you for all the coffee meetups, book recommendations, and movie dates.

Rachel Buckland: Ten years of friendship and look at us now. Thank you for being there and always ready to make me laugh.

Breann Balser: For the fanfiction and the texts.

Kate Langley: My home friend. Thank you for being the one who gets me, for being the friend who'll turn up "Fancy" and sing along to Reba louder than anyone, and for the fantastic author photo.

Twitter friends who supported me in the early days of querying and publishing and beyond. Forever grateful for your support, hand-holding, anxiety lessening, and meme sending Katie Locke, E. K. Johnston, Ashley Poston, Rachel Simon, Dahlia Adler, Tess Sharpe, S. Jae-Jones, Amy Spalding, Kip Wilson, and countless others.

Lara Ameen, Alex Gino, Emily S. Keyes, Katie Locke, Ashley Poston, Rachel Simon: For your insight and enthusiasm for early and later drafts of this book, and for helping me make it as good as possible.

Shveta Thakrar, Karuna Riazi, and Gabe Novoa: For being the best writing support group I could ask for.

Much love to the Lambda YA Cohort of 2017.

Camryn Garrett: Thank you for late night texts about publishing woes, your late-night texts about literally everything, and your love for my cat.

I cut my writing teeth on fanfiction and it still remains one of my favorite things to write. Much love to Grace, Sam, and the rest of the Wicked Gelphie fandom, and the X-Files fandom on Tumblr as well.

Dave Limburg, for being gracious with my late assignments because I had a book to write. Vielen Dank, für alles.

Risa Applegarth, Dena Coward, Jennifer Eddins, Jennifer Feather, María Sánchez, and Karen Weyler: My English teachers/professors in high school and beyond. Thank you for your support, your teaching, and for not being too upset when I hid a book behind my textbook to read during class.

In memory of my Nana, who read with me.